THE MARK OF MERLIN

OTHER WILDSIDE PRESS BOOKS
BY ANNE McCAFFREY

Ring of Fear
Cooking Out of This World (Editor)

MORE FICTION FROM WILDSIDE PRESS

Becky Barker

Impossible Match
Sassy Lady
Captured by a Cowboy
Bedroom Eyes
Back in His Arms
Renegade Texan

Lillian Stewart Carl

Memory and Desire
Shadows in Scarlet

Leonore Dvorkin

Apart from You

Roby James

The Soldier's Daughter

Laura Leone

Sleight of Hand
Ulterior Motives
The Bandit King
The Black Sheep
A Wilder Name
A Woman's Work
Untouched by Man

THE MARK OF MERLIN

Anne McCaffrey

Wildside Press

THE MARK OF MERLIN

Published by
Wildside Press
P.O. Box 301
Holicong, PA 18928-0301
www.wildsidepress.com

First Wildside Press edition: June 2002.

1

I WAS AWARE that I should be more grateful. The train was after all headed in the right direction. Track was laid from Boston to the end of Cape Cod and eventually this train, too, would arrive at its destination. Maybe not on the day of embarkation, March 18, 1945, but sometime. Such vague reassurance didn't make the journey from Boston to East Orleans in a frigid baggage car any less cold and dreary.

Not that this was the first trip I had made in a baggage car. Merlin and I had traveled that way all over the United States, including the territory of Alaska. But this time the ignominy of forcing a gentleman like Merlin among common crates, bales, and boxes, and having to have him muzzled and chained, was one more insult to the injuries of spirit I had already sustained. My rebellion was complete. The only living thing it did not touch was Merlin. He was, all totaled, the one being who cared for me, Carlysle Murdock. I should say, James Carlysle Murdock, driving that particular thorn deeper into my side.

Merlin sensed my rising inner turmoil and whined sympathetically, his tongue cramped up against the confines of that indecent muzzle. At Merlin's remark, the imbecilic baggageman cast a nervous look in our direction. I ignored him. As I had ignored his attempt to bully me into confining Merlin in a cage.

I knew how useless it was to explain that Merlin had had the benefit of schooling under the leading canine trainers in the world. That he had far better manners than three-fourths the travelers today, including service personnel. Merlin's size and his breed predisposed people immediately against him. It is difficult, I agree, to reassure the timid that one hundred and twenty pounds of silver-black German shepherd was in actual fact a driveling coward. I could show his K-9 papers discharging him on the ground of "insufficiently aggressive behavior," and I would find people ready to discredit the word of the undersecretary of war.

Oh, I could have caged him and sat forward in comfort and warmth with the human passengers, but some perverse streak in me reveled in the martyrdom of this segregation. I knew I was acting childishly, that I was not adhering to the strict "chin-up" code in which I had been raised, but that was another facet of this whole humiliating, terrible journey.

Tears, never far from my eyes these days, dribbled down my cheeks. Rather than let the baggageman misconstrue my weakness, I buried my head in Merlin's ruff, choking back the lump in my throat. Merlin's soft whine was more understanding than all the sympathy of the dean and the hospital staff at college, or the commiseration of my boardinghouse colleagues. None of these people had ever met my father, so how did they know how much I was going to miss him? How could they understand this crushing loneliness that overwhelmed me?

Here I was, sick with grief and not yet recovered from the strep throat infection that had stricken me at midterms, advised by the dean to take the rest of the spring term off "to get my bearings," on my way to meet a guardian whom I earnestly wished to hell.

And he had perpetrated the final indignity. He had not even had the grace to come get me, though he had certainly known from the dean's letter how sick I had been. I refused to allow him the one benefit of doubt to which I knew, in my heart, he was entitled. He did, after all, believe me to be a boy. Who wouldn't? With a name like James Carlysle Murdock? Was he in for a surprise! And, damn my dear father anyway, not only for inflicting such a name on me in the first place, but for not explaining to the friend he had happily conned into "guardianing" me that his beloved Carlysle—Dad had never called me "Carla" as my friends did—was actually a girl and not a boy. Major Regan Laird was in for a mighty big surprise at the station at Orleans. That is, if he condescended to come meet me there!

Remember, my better half reminded me, he's just been invalided home himself. He might not be able to drive, assuming first he has a car, and second he is able to wheedle gas out of the local ration board.

I was not to be mollified so easily. I was bound and determined to be as miserable, disagreeable, and awful as I could. That would repay the much decorated Major Regan Laird for his ridiculous letters, urging me to join the service and finish my college later.

"Apply for O.C.S. and be a credit to your father!" Indeed. What did the service ever do for Dad but kill him?

"Enlistees have tangible advantages over draftees." Sure, Major, but I'd love to see your face signing a WAC application form as my guardian. I smiled to myself, smugly sure of startling the hell out of the patronizing, insufferable, egocentric major-my-guardian.

What had my father been thinking of? Couldn't he have appointed someone I knew? Captain Erskine, for instance: He was in Fort Jay. For a year I could even put up with simpering Alice Erskine. But this unknown major? That rankled!

Now, said myself to me, your father had been mentioning this Major Laird ever since he wangled Laird's transfer to his own regiment. Laird had been praised, appreciated, blessed by Dad for two years. Two soulmates, that's what my father and the major had been. Two minds but with a single preoccupation—infantry: the proper disposition and use thereof in battle.

If it did nothing else for me, this line of thought kept me so agitated I did not feel that damp, raw sea-cold that seeped through the ill-closed baggage door as the train bucked and squealed slowly over the icy tracks. I heard the conductor calling "Yannis" at the next station. Not bad. A mere three hours late to Hyannis. Chatham would be next and finally, at long overdue last, Orleans. This endless journey to the long-delayed meeting with my unknown guardian was drawing to its conclusion.

I leaned into Merlin's warm body as the baggage master swung open the door to the icy March evening. No appreciable effort had been made here to clear the depot or the street visible just beyond. Drifts were piled high around the baggage en-trance; a narrow aisle, shovel-width, led to the passenger side of the station. Two Railway Express trucks were backed into four-foot drifts and a green mail truck was revving its motor noisily, gusts of its exhaust odors mingling with the smell of overheated oily steam drifting back from the hardworking en-gine. My stomach churned spasmodically.

Immersed in this slough of self-pity, I envisioned myself trudging drearily, freezing cold, down the deserted snowheaped streets of Orleans, trying to find my way to Major Laird's house, Merlin, his silvery coat white with snow, pacing wolflike behind me.

"Gawd, what is it? A wolf?" a masculine voice demanded in a broad down-east twang as the door creaked wide.

"Nar, the gul's dawg," the baggageman said, giving me a dirtier look than usual. He had been questioned at every stop and was as irritated by now as I.

"Should be caged. Reg'lations."

Before the baggageman could open his mouth with another of his simpleton remarks, I answered.

"They don't build cages that big."

"Bulieve it. Better keep that 'un chained down heyah, miss. Someone'll shoot 'm fer a wuff. Would indeed."

"He never leaves my side," I replied coldly, looping one arm loyally around Merlin's neck. He had watched the exchange, cocking his head right and left, ears pricking forward. He looked soulfully up at me and tried to lick his lips through the muzzle. Frustrated, he stretched his front paws out and eased his huge barrel down, resting his insultingly packaged head on his front legs.

There was the usual endless routine of waybills and did Mrs. Parson's package make this train and when did they ex-pect the shipment of Brown's and so on and on. I supposed ac-idly to myself that without the summer visitors to gossip about they had to make do with such banal topics. But it was driving me nuts. I didn't want to get to Orleans and yet I couldn't wait to confound Major Laird. I was supremely tired of train riding. I was thoroughly bored with baggage cars and I was exhausted, very cold and very hungry. Since we'd left South Station in Boston at eleven this morning I had had one single cup of lousy coffee and nothing else. The moron of a baggageman wouldn't let me leave Merlin long enough to get so much as a sandwich.

The raw sea-cold chilled me despite ski pants, boots, and heavy mackinaw. I felt deprived of muscle and bone; I was a frozen amalgam of tissue, supported upright by solid ice particles within. I had to admit that the college doctor and the dean were correct in their insistence on a term-long convalescence. I had driven myself too hard at my studies, using them to dull my senses to the fact of my father's death and my awareness of the loss of all familial relationship. I would rest now, hole up in the major's lair, and come back for the summer term. It would be asinine to suffer the defeat of poor grades when I had made dean's list every term so far.

I forced myself to ignore the exchange of platitudes between railroad officials until the baggage car was finally closed and I heard the conductor's muffled "Ar board. . . ."

Surprisingly, the train picked up speed between Hyannis and Chatham. And *mirabile dictu* there were only two crates to be unloaded at that small town. Either the threat of Nazi submarines had scared fishers inland to war plants or everyone was too poor to buy a thing. I didn't really pursue the blessing.

"Ohleens, next," the conductor intoned and I could see relief parade across the baggageman's face. He even went so far as to assemble my battered bags at the rattling door to make it easier to speed his departing guest.

"That's very kind of you," I said so sweetly he didn't get the sarcasm and mumbled a "You're welcome."

Merlin sensed the end of the journey and rose, stretching with majestic indolence. The baggageman made a strategic withdrawal to the far side of the car.

The train jolted to a stop, braked wheels spinning on the icy track. As the baggageman threw open the door, I slipped off the hateful muzzle and hand-signaled Merlin out of the car. The look of pure terror on the man's face as Merlin, free, darted out, made up for some of the indignities we had endured according to the gospel of regulations. Merlin plunged around in the snow, tail lashing with pleasure at liberty. I jumped down from the lip of the baggage car, disdaining the help of the station keeper. I pushed him aside discourteously, lifting my bags down and staggering with them to the corner of the station which seemed somewhat protected from the winds. It was snowing heavily again and the wind gusted it like sand, hard and cold, into my face. I signaled Merlin to stay by the bags. I didn't want him disappearing in a strange town on a stormy night no matter how much he needed some exercise.

The stationman and the baggageman were already deep in their endless trivia. The wind blew to fragments most of their sentences about soggy mailbags and frozen parcel posts. I peered up and down the platform, straining to see through the blown snow. In spite of my inner conversations, I knew I had counted heavily on the major meeting us. But there was no one in sight. As the wind tore at my legs, I felt the additional chill of disappointment. A heavy woman, muffled in a Hudson Bay blanket coat of ancient vintage, struggled down the high steps of the single passenger car and trudged through the snow to the street. She ducked awkwardly under the roadguard and disappeared into the wind-driven snow and darkness.

Lights shone from a taxi office, a restaurant, and a stationery store lining the far side of the snowy street. Behind the station on my side of the road I could discern the cheerful snowclad rectangles and crosses of the town's old cemetery. A lone truck stood outside the store but, as far as I could see in the darkness beyond, the street was empty of vehicles and pedestrians.

I swallowed against the pressure of more ridiculous tears. It would spoil my confrontation with the major completely if he were to find me weeping childishly. The sense of desolation and frightful loneliness was intense.

Merlin whined and rocked back and forth, yearning to break position. My gratitude for his company, much less his empathy, routed the tears. Merlin didn't need explanations. Merlin was never away when I needed him. Yet had he been as wise as his namesake, he was still not a human and his wordless sympathy was not quite enough. Although God knows, I had no other.

So complete was the sense of abandonment that self-pity deserted me. I tried desperately to find excuses for the major's absence. I had written him a week ago to confirm my coming. This morning I had wired him from South Station to expect me. I had to admit the train was a trifling matter of three hours and twenty-five minutes late but the weather was atrocious enough to account for a far longer delay. He would surely have had sense enough to call the station and check the e.t.a.

Well, I argued, he might not have a phone. He might have waited for hours and then gone home. It was past seven. No, he had gone home to eat and would be back. Home! How could I conceivably call the major's house "home"? I was an army brat. Home was where my hat was, nowhere else. No, home was where Merlin was, I amended.

Perhaps the major didn't have a car. I swung around toward the taxi stand. It was empty. Perhaps it had gone for him now the train was finally in. And if the major did have a car, it was possible, entirely probable, that he might have had engine trouble in this weather. Or got stuck in a drift on his way here. There were umpteen dozen reasons why the major was not here. None of them made much difference to the sick, cold, frightened lump in the pit of my empty, churning stomach.

The train started up and pulled out of the station with metallic complaints about the effort required to pull its half frozen cars along the icy rails. The roadguard went up. I peered into the gloom on the other side of the track and saw only the dark hulks of cars parked in the station lot. Just then I heard the station door open and shut with a bang. A figure came charging up to the station master who was wrestling with the frozen mail sacks.

"Any passengers get off, Mr. Barnstable?" a muffled voice asked.

"Jist Miz Brewster, and a gal and a big dawg from the baggage car." The stationman brushed by the figure with an apology, hurrying to get himself and his unwieldy sacks into the warmth.

The other man was the major. His stance was unmistakably military despite his bulky clothing. The relief I felt at knowing he had met the train was mingled unpleasantly with the distressing fact that he was not looking for a girl, or a girl with a dawg, and he was not happy.

"Damn young squirt's missed the train after all." His voice drifted towards me. He caught sight of me and hesitated, undecided by the sexless figure bundled in pants and mackinaw. Merlin whined and the major stamped back around the corner of the station. Just as he passed from my view, the flood of light from the window caught his face briefly. I was glad, then, that I was a distance from him, that the gusty wind covered my gasp of shock at the sight of his ruined face. Shrapnel, more than likely, had gouged through cheek and jaw. Raw heavy scar tissue drew the right eye down at the corner and twisted the mouth into a permanent half smile. No wonder he had never mentioned the nature of his wounds. No wonder he had not wanted to come to Cambridge to meet me. All plans for petty vengeance disappeared from my mind.

"Major Laird," I cried, hurrying across the intervening space.

He stopped and turned, his hand already on the doorknob. This time I saw the other half of his face and experienced a second shock. It was obvious that the major had been a handsome man. Plastic surgery would repair most of the cruel scar on the right but that anyone, man or woman, should have to endure, however briefly, such disfigurement was the other side of enough.

He said nothing but waited till I reached him. Nor did he make any move to obscure the damaged profile as he faced me.

"Major Laird," I began and impulsively thrust out my hand, "I'm Carla Murdock."

His eyes narrowed angrily and he frowned; at least, one side of his face frowned.

"Is this some kind of a joke?" he snapped.

"No, no joke," I hurried to say. "At least, not on you. If there is a joke, it's on father for having a girl and giving her the name he planned for his firstborn son, James Carlysle Murdock."

I resisted the impulse, prompted by the disbelief on his face, to reach into my shoulder bag and drag out the dog-eared birth certificate, the baptismal papers, and the sworn statement of the commandant of Fort Bragg, addressed to all draft boards, that I was legally James Carlysle Murdock and un-equivocally female.

He stared intensely at me as I was sure he had stared at in-competent junior officers and privates. Only I had seen my fa-ther use this unnerving technique too often to dissolve into the nervous stammer of self-defense it usually provoked.

"You had your fun, didn't you?" he said finally in a cold scornful voice. I knew he meant the letters he had written to an unknown boy. It would have been far more polite of me to have disabused him of his error immediately.

"And why this lie about going to Harvard?"

"I do go to Harvard. Radcliffe College is a college of Har-vard University," I retorted, stung out of remorse by his unfair accusations.

"Your mailing address. . . ."

"I can't live on campus . . . with him." I pointed at Merlin. He interpreted the gesture as a release and came over.

"That doesn't excuse you from deliberately misleading me."

"You misled yourself," I snapped, trying to keep my teeth from chattering. "My father may have called me Carlysle but I'll bet at some time or other he had to use the female pronoun. You just didn't hear. You just didn't think, mister. Most of all, you wouldn't want to be a guardian to a girl! Sweet suffering Pete," I cried, "do you think I haven't wanted to be a boy, if only for Dad's sake?" He blinked as I unconsciously used a pet expression of my father's.

I stood glaring at him and, despite the firmest clamp on my jaws, my teeth began to chatter. Merlin whined questioningly, licking his chops, shifting his paws restlessly on the snowy platform. Almost absentmindedly, the major held out a gloved hand for Merlin to sniff and as offhandedly patted Merlin's head. .

"We can't stand here all night. You'll have to come with me now," the major said. "I'll decide what to do later."

He pulled me around, a rough hand under my elbow, and pointed towards the blurred but unmistakable outline of a jeep in the parking lot.

"The jeep's mine," he said, bending to pick up my suitcases. I tried to take one from him but he glared at me fiercely. "I'm not crippled," he said with a definite accent on the final word.

Rebuffed and feeling that perhaps frozen solitude was preferable to his present company, I trudged behind him to the jeep. He tossed the bags easily into the back before sliding into the driver's seat. With cold fingers, I fumbled endlessly at the stiff handle on my side. With an exclamation of exasperation he reached over and opened the door. Merlin, without order, leaped into the backseat, sitting straight up, his tongue out, watching first me, then the major. It infuriated me that Merlin appeared to have accepted the major at first sniff.

Expertly the major backed the jeep in the treacherously drifted snow. He bisected old frozen ruts and crossed the railroad track as the jeep's four-wheel drive found what traction there existed on the bad surface of the unplowed road. He waited patiently for the traffic light to change, although there wasn't anything moving anywhere on the abandoned road.

The jeep must have been standing forever in the parking lot for inside the car it was colder than outside. The isinglass curtains were none too tight and gusts of frigid air lashed in particles of snow. I sat huddled with my arms hugging my sides, trying to make myself believe I was warm. I shivered spasmodically. Whatever reception I had anticipated, I had got more than I'd planned. Actually I never had gone beyond the first moment when the major discovered my sex. That's the problem with daydreams. They are not the least bit practical.

In all honesty I had to admit that the major had more justice on his side. I had had fun deliberately encouraging his misconception. Based on his information, he had given good advice in suggesting that his ward join the army. Faced with an inevitable draft, it would be smart for a young man to volunteer. The Allies had broken out of the Belgian Bulge and were racing across Germany to meet up with the Russian forces. Undoubtedly the war in Europe would end by spring. Then the entire concentration of Allied military strength would sweep over the Japanese positions and end the Pacific campaign. A man joining the service right now would get through basic and probably have a short tour on occupation forces. Then he'd have the G.I. Bill to see him through college.

I now realized that the major had very carefully thought out that first letter of condolence to a boy suddenly orphaned. It had been a kind letter, if devoid of emotion. He had, bluntly it is true, described the fatal injury my father had received on a routine trip at night between his command post and a bivouac he wanted to inspect. The major had gone into detail about the brief ceremony in the little Lutheran cemetery at Siersdorf where my father had been buried. Every man in the regiment who was not on duty had crowded in. The description might have read like the orders of the day but the picture evoked had been equally clear. The major had gone on to ask me what my immediate expenses were and how much I would need to finish the term. I was not to worry about staying in college, if that was what I wanted. He hadn't seen my father's will yet, but there would be enough in the National Service Insurance to see to my education. If I had damned the major for insensitivity to my grieving I had done him an injustice, for he had done the courtesy of assuming the boy was a man. I knew, now I had seen the major, that he would have written an entirely different letter had he known I was a girl.

However, neither of us had entertained the possibility that he too might be wounded or that I would work myself into ill health. Dad had been killed November 18, 1944. The major was critically wounded on December 7 in the Sportplatz near Julich. I hadn't known of that until mid-January when he wrote me from an English convalescent camp. Neither of us had thought of meeting before the summer when he expected to have enough points to get home. Now here we were, thrust together in late March under the worst of conditions.

I like to think that had he not been wounded, had I not gotten ill, I would have soon told him the truth. It was spiteful of me not to have told him. Whatever excuse I might hide behind, the fact remained I had put myself in a very bad light. My egotism had inflicted hurt on someone already badly injured. I was deeply ashamed of myself and I could think of no immediate way of convincing the major of that.

How he found his way I do not know for the full dark of deep winter was further complicated by the wind-driven snow, lowering visibility to a point just a few inches beyond the slitted headlights. The jeep growled in low gear as he inched it along. We had the road to ourselves. There weren't so much as tire marks from previous travelers to guide us for the wind swept continually over the road.

Major Laird didn't swear to himself as Dad would have, driving under such conditions. Against the isinglass window his profile was silhouetted boldly, the disfigurement hidden in the gloom. It was a strong face, dominated by an aquiline nose and a sweeping jawline, the sternness alleviated by a sensitive mouth and a full, sensuous lower lip. He was a lot more man than what drifted around campus at Harvard.

I cast about in my mind, trying to think of something to say, some way to apologize, but I was sensible enough to realize his mood was unreceptive and the conditions of the night made silence valuable. I noticed he kept glancing down at the dashboard.

"I've either overshot the turn in this foul weather or it's just ahead. You'll have to walk point till we find that blank cross-road. It's an oblique right."

You don't argue with orders given in that tone of voice. Not if you're army raised. It doesn't matter that you're cold already. He knows that, because he is, too. It doesn't matter you're not quite over a bad illness and this could make you sicker. He's taken that into consideration. I just got out and, with one hand on the right headlight, walked along the side of the road, peering through the sudden flurries, making out the black looming boxes of houses, the half-covered telephone poles, match-slim, until, fortunately not too far ahead of us, I found the turn. The brief walk had been stimulating. My toes burned and my fingers tingled. When I got back into the car, Merlin nuzzled my ear, crooning softly, deep in his throat.

The jeep proceeded a little faster until we reached another point predetermined by the odometer. Laird stopped the car and turned his head expectantly towards me. I got out, not even irritated with him when he held Merlin back from joining me. At the next crossroads we bore right again.

This road, even in the obscuring snow, had a different character: no houses, no trees, but, despite gusty winds, visibility improved. I could sense openness, could occasionally trace the horizon by the difference of the gray-white of land, the gray-black of wintry sky. Far on the left I caught a vagrant gleam of light quickly extinguished, for all Cape Cod observed strict blackout precautions. Once on the downslope to the right, I made out the tossing field of sea as it sent tentative fingers up coves on the forearm of Cape Cod. The road dipped here and there and we had to gun the car through drifts at the bottom. Sometimes the top of the road was swept clear, down to the macadam. Bay bushes thrust stark branches out to reflect the yellow slits of headlight. I don't know how far we went along this road. It must have been some distance for the warmth exercise had generated in my hands and feet had dissipated. The snow, constantly thrown against the windshield, had a mesmeric quality to it. The crow-flight distance from Orleans to Pull-in Point was approximately eight miles, and only ten by road under normal conditions. No self-respecting crow was a-wing and these were not normal conditions. I only know that it had been about seven when the train pulled into the station. When we finally entered the kitchen, the clock said eight thirty-five.

I had one more short march as point for the final left-hand turn to Pull-in Point Road above Nauset Beach. The Laird house, which in fair weather had a full view of the sea over the tops of Nauset's then substantial dunes, was partially protected by the lay of the land from the full brunt of the blizzard. Now its slanting saltbox roof was heavily laden with the accumulation of several snowstorms. It loomed blackly to our left, a solid bulk against the surrounding grayness.

"Find the driveway. There's a post on the right-hand edge to guide you."

I had trouble unbending my cramped knees. I got out very slowly, very stiffly. I came close to falling onto the post. Merlin bolted out the door as if he understood we had reached our destination. He promptly left a message at the beachplum bushes that formed the front hedge. As he barked ecstatically, snapping at the falling snow and rolling in it puppyishly, Major Laird revved the jeep for the dash up the rise to the garage I now distinguished in the gloom.

The major succeeded the second time. He gunned the motor peremptorily, recalling me to my senses, gesturing at the garage door. I slipped several times in the drifts, spitting out snow and cursing it as it leaked into my gloves and up my sleeves. I got a grip on the door handle and yanked. The top-hinged door stayed stubbornly shut. I made several more futile attempts and finally turned to the major, stretching my hands out in a show of helplessness. I heard him cursing with disgust as he crawled down from the jeep. There was some consolation in the fact that it took both of us, kicking and tugging, to loosen the frozen door.

He gave me a push towards the door in the rear of the garage. Unquestioningly I stumbled towards it as he drove the car in. My wet gloves slipped on the doorknob but I got it open the second time, gasping as warmth and light hit my face.

I lurched stiffly in, my entry hampered by Merlin who had had enough of playing around in the cold and barged past me. We entered a small back hall filled with fishing gear, hunting paraphernalia, oars, a well-greased motor, an imposing pile of cordwood, heavy-weather boots, and a filled meat safe high on the wall.

"Go on in," the major ordered impatiently as I blocked his way to warmth.

I hastily opened the door and entered a welcoming kitchen. I hurried over to the huge black wood stove, drawn like a needle by the magnet of its heat-radiating bulk. A Dutch oven squatted at the back of the range and from it came the odor of rich meat stew. Turning to present the rear of me to the stove, I saw the major clump into a corridor. I found later that it ran along the back of the house, separating the kitchen, bathroom, and a small study from the living room, dining room, and front hall. From where I stood by the hot stove I could see only doors and an area for coats and boots.

The major beckoned to me. "Hang your wet things out here," he said, less a suggestion than an order.

Mechanically I obeyed, fumbling with the ski-boot fastenings. My other shoes were in the suitcases which he placed just inside the dining room. I decided it was too much effort to rummage through the luggage for mere shoes. I got my boots off. My socks were either very wet or very cold; my toes were too numb to know the difference. I hung up my heavy mackinaw and scarf and walked like an automaton back to the kitchen. I sat stiffly down at the old honey-colored table in the chair nearest the stove.

The major had filled two plates with stew and two mugs with coffee from a pot that had also been kept warm at the back of the stove. He served me and himself, then ladled out another bowl, splashing it with water to cool it quickly. He put this down by the hall door and whistled. .

Merlin had gone on his own private reconnaissance through the house and, although he had never been whistled at in that particular arpeggio, he knew he was being paged. I heard his claws clicking against bare floors. He came into the kitchen, head high, eyes curious, darting, taking in everything in a sweeping gaze. He looked up at the major, at me, and then went to the bowl of food. He sniffed at it and sat down, tongue hanging out.

"Eat, Merlin," I said and he rose and approached the food in earnest.

I had made it a point that Merlin should never accept food without my permission. I had trained him this way after two of his litter brothers were poisoned "by person or persons un-known." Ha! I'd known. The disadvantage to this discipline was that I could not leave Merlin for more than forty-eight hours. He simply would not eat. When the strep throat had been at its worst and I was delirious, Merlin had stubbornly fasted for four days. Then one of my friends had brought him to the window outside the infirmary. Receiving my permission, though how he recognized me by the croak my voice had become I don't know, the poor dog had wolfed down three pounds of horsemeat.

Right now he acted equally starved and I realized how hungry I was. Part of my depression must be due as much to hunger as cold. The stew had simmered into a semisolid mass, tasty, hot, restoring. The coffee, like any respectable army brew, was strong enough to have floated the stove. I cleaned my plate twice and felt infinitely more like facing the problem of the major.

In my concentration on the meal I had said nothing to him and had managed to forget his existence beyond the click of silverware against china. My attention was drawn back to him when a pack of cigarettes was thrust under my nose.

"Smoke?"

"I don't."

He lit one, the smoke he exhaled shadowing briefly the injured cheek. His look, without the disfiguration, would have been somber enough. I noticed that his hand bore scars, too, and I later learned that he had taken mine fragments all through the right arm and chest. He had, it turned out, been trying to drag the man in front of him out of the minefield.

"The situation is this, Miss Murdock," he said bluntly, leaning forward slightly. "It was perfectly all right for me to extend hospitality to my male ward of twenty. Quite another thing when that ward is female. There is no one in the house but me. And while this may be wartime, there are still proprieties to be observed."

"But . . . we barely made it here," I exclaimed, gesturing out at the whirling night.

He shook his head impatiently. "Not tonight, of course, you idiot. I'll find a place in the village tomorrow."

"I'm sorry I was so silly not to tell you," I babbled, unable to meet his eyes. "And I'll be twenty-one in less than a year so you won't be bothered with me long. Oh, the whole thing is ridiculous," I cried, jumping up, annoyed because I couldn't even make a decent apology to him.

He looked up at me with less rancor. He reached out one hand and reseated me.

"It's not that I am bothered with you, my dear ward. To be truthful, I couldn't do enough to repay the debt I owe Jim—your father. It's just that it would be so much easier if you were a boy."

"That's what father always said," I muttered sullenly.

"You make a much prettier girl . . . or would if you had some flesh on you. That dean didn't exaggerate when she said you were run down."

"Her!" I grated out between my teeth. I'd had my run-ins with crab-eyes. Some of my resentment must have been reflected in my expression for he suddenly smiled at me.

"From the tone of her letter, I gather she considered me her contemporary," he remarked dryly.

"Fatherly and white-haired, suitable guardian to a well brought-up army brat," I replied in a simpering voice, up to the last two words which I spat out.

"Brat is right," he agreed firmly. "And as your guardian and by the few gray hairs I possess as of this moment, you get to bed."

"It isn't even ten yet," I complained, glancing at the clock.

"The time is immaterial, the way you look. I'll show you your room."

"The way I look indeed," I murmured to myself but I followed him.

"Which bag do you need tonight?" he asked and I pointed.

He led the way through the corridor into the dining room, to the front hall beyond. As I entered the foyer, I saw on my left the most unusually lovely stairway I have ever seen. A short flight of steps, parallel to the front door, ended on a low landing where the stairs continued, again parallel to the front door, to an intermediate landing, then switched on a short leg of a Z to the upper level. The balustrade over the stairwell was slightly bowed out, the spindles gracefully and unusually turned. It was a clever variation which fitted into a smaller space than conventional flights.

Major Laird noticed my surprise and pointed out the chandelier hanging over the stairwell.

"I mean to get the house electrified one day but not that. With candles in it, it is lovely to behold. Electricity would spoil it. This house is fairly old, added onto during the course of the eighteen hundreds. The oldest part is between the kitchen and the garage. I'll show you tomorrow."

We climbed the stairs and I stopped at each level, turning to see the effect.

The major shoved open an H-hinged door into a room at the front of the house, to the right of the stairs. Merlin padded in ahead and circled the room. The major ducked mechanically where the roof sloped down in front of the house. He lit the kerosene light on a massive old cherry bureau and laid my case at the foot of the four-poster spool bed with its quilted coverlet.

"It's a lovely room," I murmured, glancing around at the sparse but good furnishings, noticing the handmade braided rugs on the wide planked floors.

"My mother enjoyed this sort of stuff," he commented, implying that he did not.

"Bathroom's down the hall, second door on the right. Colder'n Croesus, I warn you. No way to heat it." He turned to the fireplace in this room, its coals glowing warmly. He threw on more wood and the fire flared up obediently.

"More blankets in here if you're cold," he told me, tapping the blanket chest at the foot of the bed.

I sat down wearily on the high bed. Merlin jumped up and I was about to order him down, looking up at the major apprehensively. Even if he didn't approve of the antiques, he might not want a dog on his mother's patchwork quilt.

"I wish I had him to keep me warm tonight," he said, grinning ruefully as he closed the door behind him. He stuck his head back in. "We're on total blackout here, so keep your curtains drawn."

"In a blizzard?"

"In a blizzard!"

I waited until I heard his footsteps on the stairs. Fatigue seeped through me. I pulled myself up by a bedpost and struggled to open the suitcase. I found slippers and a flannel nightgown. I shed my clothes and kicked them out of my way under the bed and the hell with them tonight.

I shuddered as the cold sheets chilled me even through the heavy flannel. Merlin did his usual act of stretching out beside me. He was longer than I. His warmth spread soothingly through the heavy blankets and he squirmed on his back to get comfortable against me. His warm moist nose prodded my ear in a canine kiss. Fine life when only your dog wishes you goodnight, I thought as I closed my eyes.

2

It was a combination of the cold and the wind that roused me. And once half conscious, I felt a vague nausea develop rapidly from chronic to acute. I staggered from the bed, barely aware of my surroundings. Merlin was instantly alert, whining a concerned question. I fumbled for the door latch, managed to open the door, and ran down the hallway. The upper hall was narrow and I barely avoided tumbling down the stairs, dizzy with nausea as well as sleep.

"Second door, second door," I heard myself mumbling and swallowed against the rising substance in my gorge. I slammed open the door and saw the gleam of the toilet bowl. I just made it.

Merlin thrust an inquisitive nose at my arm and I pushed him away impatiently. He was no use to me. I heard his nails scrabbling against the bare floor. I kept on being ill. I kept on being ill and then I started to shiver, because the bathroom was colder'n Croesus. I started to shiver and I couldn't stop and it was a toss-up between shivering and dry-retching. I didn't have the strength to crawl back to bed. I huddled weakly against the toilet seat.

My eyes had just become accustomed to the dark when I caught a glimpse of light over my shoulder. I groaned at the humiliation of having the major find me in such a condition. I groaned and my teeth chattered and I retched futilely.

"God, what next?" I heard him say as he paused on the threshold. I felt his warm hand on my forehead, the skin rough with the uneven scar tissue.

"You're freezing."

I chattered back at him.

"Through being ill?"

I nodded, swallowing against the reflexive spasm that seized my diaphragm. He took my hand in his and drew me to my feet. His wool bathrobe was warm under my hands He slipped an arm under my knees and picked me up. I also cracked my head against the door frame as he maneuvered me out.

"For the love of webfooted friends in the forest," I complained. His hands tightened spasmodically on my knees and shoulder. It was another of my father's favorites.

Laird was more careful angling me into my room, but he stopped halfway in. I was shivering uncontrollably now, grabbing tightly at his neck and arm to still the shakes.

"Colder'n hell in here," he muttered and backed out.

Downstairs, through the dining room, out into the corridor he carried me, kicking open a door into what had been the original house. The room was about twenty feet square, narrow windows high in the walls just under the ceiling. A huge fireplace, its coals banked for the night, radiated tremendous warmth. As the major lowered me to the studio couch, I had a revolving impression of the doors and bookshelves and Merlin sniffing around the room.

The major covered me tightly with the blankets, holding them down against my shaking body.

"Chilled riding that goddamfool baggage car with your overgrown wolf. Made a pig of yourself with stew so what else can you expect from a half-well organism like your body," he muttered.

I tried to will myself to relax to the warmth that surrounded me. He pressed the covers more tightly to me. Then, with the queer whistle he could make without compressing his lips, he ordered Merlin up beside me. In the variable light from the dying fire his face assumed satanic qualities, the flames alternately flaring to illumine the scarred surface, then dying to cast it completely in shadow.

With a snort of impatience he turned to the fireplace. He came back with a shot glass full of liquor.

"If you haven't started drinking, you're about to learn at the insistence of your guardian." He held the glass against my lower lip and tilted it deftly, so that despite my chattering the fluid got into my mouth. I gulped it down, grateful for the burning stuff although I'm not fond of Scotch. It always tastes to me the way ants smell . . . formic acidy.

"It's a dog's dose," he remarked, "but I've got to warm you up. You're so thin you'll break bones shaking like that."

He poured another stiff drink, and disregarding my weak protest, propped my head in the crook of his arm and kept forcing the Scotch down my throat.

By the third shot I couldn't focus and I didn't bother to resist. But the shivering had stopped and I felt exceedingly warm and cozy. I was also sure that there was, somehow or other, a coating of ice, smooth and unbreakable, over my entire body. I told him so. I suggested that he stand me upright in the fireplace. If I put my head in the chimney I'd fit and then the ice would melt before I could get burned.

I remember he had a very pleasant laugh which was the first pleasant thing I had noticed about him. I told him so and was rewarded by another laugh. Something caught me by the back of the neck in one convulsing jerk and I remember that he held me against him and patted my head gently. He talked about a girl who had a curl in the middle of her forehead. I felt insulted enough to point out that I had too damned many curls all over my head and he was welcome to all he wanted to help hide his scar. I remember his hand over my mouth and that I was very very warm and very very sleepy.

Something heavy lay across my chest and my right arm was asleep. I woke up. I must not have been completely sober at that point because I looked down, quite calmly, at the major's arm across my breasts. It didn't seem at all improper that I was in the same bed with him because I was warm. This had been terribly important some long past time ago.

A kerosene lamp, flickering as the wick used up the last of the fuel in the well, gave a feeble light from the shelf over our heads. The major's pajama sleeve had slid up and I could see the terrible gashes, rawly red, where shrapnel had sliced through the fleshy part of the arm. Yet his hand was long-fingered, well shaped, and strong, the nails flat, deep, and well kept. My father had always watched a man's hands as he saluted or shook, not the face. Dad always maintained he could separate men into categories by the shape and care they too of their hands.

Regan Laird would surely have passed that test with honors. So his face didn't matter and the surgeons would work their minor miracles and put him back together again. In repose his right profile lost some of the distortion it had in waking. The eye did not seem so drawn nor the grin such a travesty. He had lost half his right eyebrow, which gave him a curiously bald look. The scar tissue extended up into the hairline but his thick black hair had been carefully cut to hide most of it. The worst furrows of keloidal tissue stretched across the cheekbone down to the jawline. I remember my father mentioning how Regan took care of the petticoat problems in the regiment. An ambiguous statement. Now I had seen the major's good side, I imagined all manner of interpretations.

Scarred or not, Regan Laird was *muy hombre* as Turtle Bailey would have said in that gravel-pit voice of his. So different, I sighed to myself, from what infested the campus. Irresistibly tempted, I carefully twitched a long piece of hair away before it ticked his nose and roused him. His hair was unexpectedly fine and silky under my fingers and, feeling foolish, I stroked his hair back over the scar. He moved and, startled, I withdrew my hand. But I didn't remove the arm he had thrown across me. Big warm heavy Merlin was firmly planted along my left side so I was wedged between two male bodies. Would Merlin constitute a chaperon in Mrs. Grundy's eyes, I wondered?

The kerosene lamp flickered and went out. The quiet hiss of the fire lulled me. Warm and feeling safe for the first time since Dad had shipped out three years before, I slept.

A LOUD CRACK-POP woke me. A log had split on the fire. I looked around, startled to find neither the major nor Merlin in the room. The kerosene lamp, filled and trimmed, burned brightly on the shelf. Gray light filtered in from the high windows, the gray light of a stormy day, not early morning.

I was warm but the memory of last night's chill had not receded far enough for me to want to rise from the comfort of the bed. I heard Merlin's nails clicking. I heard a door open to the accompaniment of Merlin's glad barking. I pictured him outside, trying to bite snowflakes, leaping and twisting his big frame in an awkward return to puppyhood. I imagined him sniffcasing the yard, leaving "sign" on every likely bush and stone.

The door to the back hall opened, letting in a billow of frigid air. The major entered, his hands occupied with a tray, adroitly kicking the door closed with a deft foot.

"Is there anything that dog doesn't know about you?"

"Hmmm?"

"He's been sitting in front of the door for the last hour," the major explained as I struggled to a sitting position so he could put the tray on my lap.

"Tea?" I cried in horror.

"Better for your stomach after last night. Yes, Merlin told me in plain language you were awake. He considered he could be relieved of sentry duty and he wanted out."

I grinned at the major.

"Dad always said Merlin had more sense than most sergeants, even if he didn't take to K-9 training."

The major raised his left eyebrow questioningly. The right one did not move. His face, plainly visible in the daylight, did not seem so grotesque. I suppose you can get used to anything to the point where you don't even see it.

"Yes," I went on, stirring plenty of sugar in the tea to take the curse off it, "Merlin chickened out of K-9 training. He wouldn't attack."

"'Damn all sugar in our tea?'" the major asked, pointedly watching the teaspoonfuls I ladled into the cup. "So they discharged him, huh?"

"Yes, insufficiently aggressive for active duty was the euphemism. Dad said the dog had too much sense to attack a stuffed dummy that hadn't done anything. Merlin is fast enough if a live 'un raises a gun, though."

Major Laird snorted sympathy for the fine distinction.

"I might not believe you if I hadn't seen his performance this morning. But I do. I'm sure I'll agree more as our acquaintance deepens. But the dog must have complicated your life no end. No, eat all of it!"

"I don't like eggs in the morning," I said enunciating clearly. "Particularly soft-boiled eggs."

"I don't care what you don't like. This diet is designed to re-introduce your stomach to solids. I've a suspicion you ignored all basic convalescent rules, or you wouldn't have got so ill last night."

"Your cooking!"

"My cooking my . . . sainted aunt," he replied, frowning as I laughed over his hurried substitution of a politer phrase But his face told me he would shove the eggs down my throat if I demurred so I gagged the mixture down, hoping it would regurgitate and annoyed because it tasted surprisingly good.

"I had quite a row with the college about Merlin," I remarked, picking up the original subject. "That's why I ended up at a boardinghouse instead of a dorm. And I had a helluva time finding—"

"You don't need to swear."

"If I feel like it, I will—a house that would accept him." I chuckled smugly. "When I was sick, Mrs. Everett was very glad he was in her house. Someone tried to burgle it twice. Merlin nearly broke the window in my room when the thief tried to get in from the roof."

The major looked at me sharply, frowning, "Into your room?"

"Eyah. My room gives onto the back porch roof."

The Major's frown deepened, on the left side, that is. "I gather Merlin dissuaded him thoroughly?"

I grimaced. "No. He got away. Now if Mrs. Everett had had the sense God gave little apples, she'd have let Merlin loose and told him to go get the man. But," and I shrugged philosophically, "she didn't and he escaped."

The major was thoughtful as he refilled my cup.

"I don't want any more."

"Immaterial. You need fluids. You're dehydrated. Stir hard. I don't mind the noise and you've two months' rations on the bottom of the cup."

"I am not dehydrated."

"Want a mirror?"

I closed my mouth with a snap and sullenly spooned more sugar in the cup, stirring with as much noise as I could make.

"Bathroom's down the corridor," the major said, throwing a heavy wool bathrobe on the bed. "You'd better stay here today. I can keep it warmer."

"But . . . I thought. . ."

"Blizzard!" and he took the tray back to the kitchen.

Snowbound with the major. How romantic! I thought acidly.

BY THE TIME I finished the second mug of oversweet tea, common sense had asserted itself. I knew that I had been outflanked and outranked and it didn't happen often enough to sit well. But I would snitch some coffee. Him and his tea! No one as thoroughly indoctrinated in army ways as I was could consider starting a day without coffee. I slid down under the covers again, gathering warmth for what was surely going to be a cold dash for a freezing bathroom.

The corridor was really frigid but not the bathroom. It backed against the kitchen and a vent from the stove kept the room, probably converted from an old shed, luxuriously warm. A huge raised tub, pull-chain toilet, and ornate lavatory indicated that someone in the Victorian era had preferred not to brave the rigors of Cape Cod winters for trips to the outhouse. I was deeply grateful. And *mirabile dictu!* hot water steamed out of the spigot. I jerked my hand back in time to avoid being scalded. I'd have preferred a bath but, in view of my weakened condition and the chilly corridor back to the warm study, decided against it. It was morally comforting to know the facilities existed.

A mirror, badly in need of resilvering, told me I was no Cinderella. As a matter of fact, I wouldn't have made it as Apple Witch. My eyes were dark holes in my face, my cheeks drawn and gaunt. Perhaps it was the effect of the shot silver. I'd never looked that desiccated before!

Men's toiletries took up the small shelf above the sink. I made bold to pull the major's comb through the tangle of my hair. Great wads pulled loose as they had ever since my fever. I'd be bald, I was sure, despite the doctor's reassurance that there would be new growth coming in. All fringe benefits of the high fever. Maybe my hair would grow back in straight, I mused hopefully, and pulled at a curl experimentally. It flopped back into place with disgusting resilience. I made a face at my reflection, which was almost an improvement. Why did my lipstick have to be up under my bed? I needed all the color could get.

When I opened the bathroom door, a smell of coffee wafted up the corridor. I could go back to the study by way of the kitchen. I had been a good girl and I had kept my eggs down. Maybe I could have coffee as a reward.

A muted thudding caught my attention and I ducked back to the window, parting the blind. The major, bundled up in a bright hunting coat, was right outside splitting kindling. H threw a piece out towards the scrub bushes for Merlin to retrieve. The major's good profile was towards me and I could see his grin, the flash of his even teeth, as he watched my idiot dog romping. Given half a chance by people who are not cowed by his size and apparent ferocity, Merlin was as agreeable companion as you'd want. The major was not the least intimidated, and Merlin was taking full advantage of the relaxed atmosphere.

I thought of Mrs. Everett who never quite trusted him in the same room with her. Merlin was always the gentleman in her house, instinctively aware of her anxiety. On campus he knew which of my classes he could sneak into, lying quietly under my chair. He also knew which lecture halls to avoid completely, returning after the hour was up to escort me home or to the next class. He had become, very shortly, as much a campus feature as the two legitimate seeing-eye dogs. He ignored them studiously. They were working.

Of course, Mrs. Everett's attitude had changed after Merlin had routed the prowler. She had even unbent enough to pat his head tentatively as she accompanied me to the taxi the day before. Day before! It seemed like years ago. Time had been suspended during that incredible train ride and that ageless drive in the jeep.

"You will be coming back, won't you, dearie?" Mrs. Everett had asked anxiously through the taxi window.

I had roomed with her for two years, summer and winter. She had been kind and comforting when she discovered my lack of family. I would always remember the terrible stricken look on her face when she brought me the telegram informing me of Dad's death. She had known instinctively what news that telegram contained. She'd had one herself for her navy son. She and Mr. Everett had done more than true relatives would have for their "poor orphaned lamb." Kay Alexander who roomed down the hall told me that's what the Everetts called me.

I was not above milking such reactions. To tell the truth, kindly boardinghouse ladies had been mother surrogates since my own had died when I was five. What none of them would admit was that I was perfectly capable of taking care of myself. Dad had seen to that. However, when I occasionally needed a female ally against some of Dad's purely masculine directives, I was bald-faced enough to use any nearby sympathetic soul to achieve the ends in mind: dating, long dresses, less childish clothes, more spending money, dancing lessons, and the rest of these absolutely essential items an army colonel could not have imagined. Consequently I had a handpicked string of courtesy aunts and uncles all over the country. There were few cities near large army installations in the United States and its territories where I could not find a roof to shelter me off base. And Dad had to name Laird my guardian!

But those people had only been buffers against Dad's idiosyncracies. He had always been there, somewhere, on maneuvers, on duty, but there. Alive. Now I was really on my own, despite the legal farce of Major Regan Laird.

I wondered how old the major was. The war had graven such terrible marks on him it was impossible to guess accurately. Late thirties? Perhaps. Old!

I heard him pounding snow off his boots on the back porch and I cleaned my hair from his comb, putting it back precisely in the military brush from which I had filched it.

I scampered down the hall, to the kitchen, hoping to snag some coffee before he reentered. He had come straight to the stove with his armload of kindling.

"Close the damn hall door, girl," he ordered as I stood there, thwarted. I slammed the door and stayed firm. He might leave.

He dumped his burden into the woodbox and poked several sticks into the stove. He glanced up and caught me staring at the coffeepot. He grinned.

"Stomach feel normal?"

I nodded.

"All right then. Fix me a cup, too. It's . . . hmmmm . . . it's cold out there and snowing again."

"Sorry to cramp your style," I remarked sweetly as I found cups in the cabinet beside the kitchen sink. I couldn't quite reach the shelf so I hoisted myself onto the counter. The major's long arm intercepted my grasp and I glared around at him.

"You are a little bit of a thing," he said, handing me the cups.

He looked at me as though seeing me clearly for the first time. He would pick right now when I looked ghastly. I tugged for him to release the cups to me. He held onto them, regarding me steadily. It was difficult for me, in returning his gaze, to re-sist the compulsion to drop my glance slightly to the furrows of his wounded cheek. He smiled, the smile echoing in his gray eyes.

"A little bit of a cocky thing," he repeated. He meant it, as Turtle Bailey, Dad's sergeant, always did, as a compliment.

He let go of the cups and, picking me up at the elbows, lifted me off the counter. "Next time, use the step stool by the door," he commented, nodding in its direction. "Like mine black and sweet."

"And we are grad-u-ally, fading away," I warbled as I poured the coffee.

Merlin, who had crawled under the table, flipped onto his side with a great groan, as if deploring my singing. He let out a huge sigh and fell asleep.

"Are we really snowbound?" I asked mischievously.

"Yes, indeed. We were damned lucky not to go off that road last night. Coast Guard had plowed, fortunately, right up to the final turnoff or I'd never have made it out. Damn train being late nearly sewed us up in town. There's only the one inn in Or-leans." He reflected a moment. "Probably been better if we had stayed there though it's no Waldorf."

"You're a good guardian, protecting my virtue," I taunted him.

"Don't kid yourself about that," he snapped, annoyed by my flippancy.

"I can take care of myself," I lashed back. "I'm a colonel's daughter and the day I can't handle a mere major . . ."

He saw the humor in the situation quicker than I did and threw back his head to laugh. He sobered as quickly.

"All kidding aside, Carlysle . . ."

"Carla," I corrected him automatically.

"I'm too used to thinking of you as 'Carlysle' and male to change both at once . . . All kidding aside, it'd be better for you not to stay on here any longer than the storm."

I got the feeling then that it was not the proprieties that

worried him. I couldn't imagine what did. Then he confirmed a nagging doubt I'd had.

"You said there were two attempts to enter your rooming house? Was it the first or second time that Merlin interfered?"

"The second. Why do you ask?"

"Oh, nothing."

"That's the kind of nothing that's something," I replied with exasperation.

He raised an eyebrow but made no explanation.

"Did you bring everything you own with you?" he asked, nodding towards the corridor where my other suitcases still lay. "Or did you leave things with Mrs. Everett?"

"I left all my college books." I grimaced sullenly. "And my summer clothes are stored in a trunk in her cellar."

"You'll be back in the summer and you'll make up this term. For Christ's sake, the dean was justified," he exploded as I turned obdurately sulky over that hotly contested decision. "You're nothing but skin and bones. Worn out. Mentally, too, I'll wager. Book fatigue, nothing more. Tired minds make mistakes and risk lives."

"I'm not in a position to risk lives," I replied angrily.

"No, you're risking more. Your education and your future."

"You know so much about it?"

He glared back at me, refusing to budge an inch. "In that letter, your dean—"

"Oh? Really, and you never tumbled from her letterhead that I was at Radcliffe, not Harvard. . . ." I sneered.

"I thought it was a wartime exigency. So many professors drafted, the Radcliffe faculty pitching in to fill the gaps. . . ."

"A likely tale. You didn't want me to be female any more than my father did."

"Damn well told," he shouted, his carefully contained temper erupting, "and it'd be a piece of infantile foolishness for you to jeopardize a dean's list record with your bullheadedness."

The fact that he was absolutely right and rational only infuriated me more. The decision had been forced on me and I resented coercion bitterly.

"You'll obey me in this, young lady. Legally I'm your guardian, and I'll decide what's right for you when you're too stubborn blind stupid to see the forest for the trees. You'll take this term off if I have to lock you up."

"I'm not in the goddamned army," I yelled, jumping to my feet.

"Too damned bad you're not. You'd've learned to obey if you were!"

There we were, both on our feet, glaring at each other, our faces inches apart. The tension reached Merlin's sleeping senses and he barked sharply twice. That brought us to our senses. I blinked at the major's angry face, the cords of his neck taut and the ridges of the keloidal tissue red and angry-looking.

I was instantly heartily ashamed at my outburst. He was assuming a disagreeable responsibility and I was being a silly little fool not to make things as easy as possible for him. I sat down abruptly, stirring my coffee vigorously.

"I'm sorry," I said, sincerely contrite. "I am behaving childishly. I'm being unfair to you. You're right. I am worn out. I'll behave."

He remained standing for a moment so I couldn't see his face. He sat down slowly. His unscarred left hand covered mine with a brief reassuring squeeze.

"I'll make an arrangement for you in town and then you'd better go back to the Everetts after I leave."

I looked at him stupidly. "After you leave?"

"I'm to report to Walter Reed in a few weeks," he said tonelessly. In spite of myself my eyes went to his scarred face. He returned my startled look expressionlessly.

"But I could stay here then."

He shook his head violently, frowning savagely.

"You can't stay here alone."

"Why not?" I insisted. "Merlin won't let anyone he doesn't know. . . ."

Major Laird closed his mouth with a snap.

"You said . . ." and he leaned forward to me, angry again, "you said you'd behave. Just leave it that I have good and sufficient reason for wanting you . . . in . . . town." He hesitated just enough to clue me he was evading. He knew I caught it but refused to give me the satisfaction of a direct answer or an explanation. I was forced to bide by my agreement to behave.

I swallowed my hasty words. I wanted to say that I was well able to take care of myself. He'd've tossed them back to me.

"How long will you be gone?" I asked instead.

He shook his head, a curt negative. I couldn't see why he wouldn't welcome the plastic surgery which surely must be the reason for his hospitalization. He couldn't like looking this way. Why else had he come to such a remote place as this? He had been a very handsome man before his injury. Vanity, self-respect alone—unless his personality had unexpectedly warped—would demand that he take advantage of a facial restoration. It was incomprehensible why he was reluctant to go to Walter Reed. I wondered if he just didn't want to leave Pull-in Point.

"When the snow stops," he said heavily, "I'll make arrangements for you in town. Or maybe over in Chatham." He gave a short mirthless laugh. "They have a movie house. Runs a show every weekend."

"And church bingo on Thursdays. Big deal!"

We finished our coffee in strained silence. The cold of the house was suddenly more preferable. I jumped to my feet, trying to act normal, and walked with unnaturally stiff legs to rinse my cup in the sink.

"I'll get dressed and wash these up," I said in a falsely bright voice as I added the mug to the stacks on the drainboard.

"I'd appreciate it," and his voice had a rueful sound. "It's rather . . . ahem . . . beneath the dignity of a major," he mocked his rank in an effort to lighten the atmosphere of the room, "to do KP."

I gave him a grin that was not too off-center normal and plunged out into the cold hall.

3

THE MAJOR had stoked up the fire in my bedroom so it was warm enough to dress. I dug out army issue longjohns and officer pinks I had had tailored for me when Dad got new uniforms just before going overseas. I forced myself not to dwell on that inadvertent association. I pulled on a green long-sleeved sweater and then a gray sweatshirt. It was too cold to be feminine. I dug out heavy socks and the mukluks Dad sent from his Alaskan inspection trip. I even had a fur parka from that jaunt, exceedingly practical for crossing frigid Cambridge common.

I set up the pictures of Dad and Mother and a couple of little mementos I always carry with me to make hotel and boarding rooms mine no matter how short a time I inhabited them. Dad, in an expansive mood, used to call me "Pussy" because I was able to make myself at home the minute I entered a new place. Turtle had taught me that flexibility and I was overwhelmed with a desire to see that old reprobate. Because he was part and parcel of my life with Dad, I crowded down that longing. Turtle was overseas anyway. I wouldn't see him till after the war. If he survived this one.

Such gloomy thoughts were disastrous and I hastily scrambled under the bed for the clothes I had thrown there last night. I made the bed and, slamming the cover down on my suitcase, felt free to leave.

I decided to do a reconnaissance of the upper floor as an antidote to my nostalgia. The first door on the right opened into another period-perfect room, dominated by a spindle four-poster bed complete with muslin canopy. I'd've moved my things right in if my relations with the major had been better. I'd wanted a four-poster canopy bed since I was a little girl.

There'd been one in a boardinghouse near Benning. I'd thought the canopy was to keep dreams in and obviously the bed was fit for a princess. For months afterwards I'd plagued Dad to get me a "princess bed." Mother'd squashed that notion the first and every time I brought it up. She hated living on post and avoided it by not having any furnishings at all. We'd always lived in boardinghouses off base. There were advantages. Army wives used to say they never made a move without losing the one valuable piece they owned or having their best china pulverized. Misdirected personal belongings were standard operating procedure so you were better off carrying what you owned with you, whenever possible.

Mother invariably managed to find temporary quarters which included my care. As a small child, I'd adored my mother—but always at a distance that wouldn't muss her dress or smudge her makeup. Now I see her as a frivolous woman, unsuited for motherhood, and selfish. I never let my father know I had overheard the gossip that mother had been killed on her way to meet another man. It had made me love my father more, excuse him his tempers and his eccentricities. Perhaps if he had loved the army less, he would have kept his wife. There I was again, reminiscing.

I closed that door and went on, looking in briefly at the bathroom. It was larger than a conventional one, so I assumed it had been added much later in the house's life. It might have originally been a nursery or a sewing room but it made a most luxurious bathroom.

The first room in the rear of the house was a catchall; cedar chests and a wardrobe I didn't investigate. I was turning to go when I saw the army footlockers. There were three, one on top of the other. The camouflaged paint pattern on one of them was strangely familiar. I walked over. The middle one. The old stenciling had been masked out with a smear of army green and the new legend gave Major Regan Laird's name, serial number, and this address. The other two were newer and obviously his but I could have sworn the middle one was my father's.

Only one small box, tucked right now in the outside pocket of my bomber bag downstairs, had come back to me, containing his most personal effects. I had assumed Turtle disposed of the uniforms and clothing. I certainly didn't want to see them again. I'd better ask the major though. There were some things of Dad's, his stamps, for instance, that had not come back yet. I'd been too ill when the first package came to pursue the matter. The major would know. I'd ask him.

There were two other bedrooms on the floor, frigid but furnished, dusty with long disuse. In the front bedroom I paused to look out the window, over the frozen drifts to the gun-green sea tossing whitecaps beyond the protecting dunes of Nauset strand. The poles of a small wharf stuck up through the snow across the way so there must be a navigable cove for the neighbors further down the Point.

A movement, barely discernible through the veil of falling snow, caught my eye. I peered out but the angle was wrong and I couldn't see far enough on the road to distinguish man, beast, or car. Just then Merlin barked.

I raced around the hall and thundered down the stairs, skidding on the bare treads in the slick-soled mukluks. Between my noise and Merlin's, the major came whipping out of the study. Merlin, tail a-wag, came bounding in from the kitchen and propped his front feet on the windowsill, craning his head, barking furiously.

"Whoever it is, Merlin knows him," I said in surprise, pointing to Merlin's lashing tail.

The major, his face anxious, leaned around Merlin's head to squint through the shifting snow.

"Whoever it is is coming here," I exclaimed.

"You must be mistaken," he said, half in anger.

"I'm not mistaken and furthermore, it's an infantryman. You can't mistake that gait," I asserted, peering through the window beside him.

The figure swung clumsy arms up and down to warm himself as he trudged head down against the swirling snow. Suddenly the angle of the head, the attitude of the whole figure were incredibly familiar. Merlin barked twice, his voice carrying through the walls into the air outside. The man stopped, looked up at the house.

I dashed for the front door, flinging it open, heedless of the snow blown in on the freezing wind.

"Turtle! In here! On the double!" I shrieked.

"Gawd, that can't be Little Bit!" Waving an arm in violent greeting, Turtle lumbered forward, floundering in the drifts, half staggering, half slipping up the incline. I would have leaped out to help him but the major grabbed my arm. Merlin leaped into the snow, raucously welcoming Sergeant Edward Turtle Bailey. I wrenched myself free of the major's grip as Turtle waddled up to the door. Flinging myself at him, I was suddenly choking on tears of relief and nostalgia. The old familiar Turtle Bailey, so constantly my father's companion, brought home at last the fact that Dad would not return from this tour of duty.

Instead of me ushering Turtle in, it was Turtle and the major carrying a hysterical me back to the fire.

"He's gone, Turtle! He's gone! He said he'd always come back and he won't! He's not going to come back this time," I wailed.

"Yessir, Bit, I know," Turtle's gravelly voice muttered, roughened by the tears that coursed down his own stubbly cheeks. He looked gray and stricken and every year of his age. The major must have taken off his overcoat because the fruit salad on Turtle's chest scratched my face as I abandoned myself to grief.

"He's not coming back! He bought it! He bought it," I cried.

"Honest, sir, this isn't like her. She was always the soldier, a regular little bit of a soldier. Even when her mother died."

Turtle's huge hands held me with great tenderness. He dabbed at my streaming cheeks with a khaki handkerchief, then blotted his own brimming eyes.

"She's been rather sick," the major murmured understandingly.

That made me blubber worse. It was all too true. Maybe that's why I broke up so completely, seeing Turtle. Dad had been out on summer war games in the wilds of southern Jersey when mother had been killed in a car accident. We'd been based at Dix. Turtle had been in the O.D.'s office on some errand from the games when the local police had called in to report the accident. It had been Turtle who had called me from a sand fight, I remember that very well, to tell me about my mother. At five, I hadn't fully understood what he had tried to explain. So naturally I hadn't cried. Now I did. Perhaps I cried for my mother, too.

"C'mon now, Bit. This ain't like you," Turtle growled. "Sick er not."

"Give her this," I heard the major say.

"Knock it back the way I taughtcha," Turtle ordered, handing me the shot glass.

Still boohooing, I looked first at the resolute major and then at an equally determined Turtle. The Scotch did the trick because I had to stop sobbing or choke. Once I could stop crying, I was thoroughly ashamed of myself. But, honestly, it was Turtle who touched it off. Certainly I'd prefer not to blubber in front of the major, my guardian, Regan Laird.

"Oh, Turtle! I'm so liquid. Major, give him a shot, too. He must be frozen. Don't tell me you slogged it all the way from the station?" I demanded, fussing in my turn over the sergeant. I pushed him into the leather chair by the fire, handed him the drink the major poured, and then started to strip off his combat boots, soaking despite their waterproofing.

"Major don't have no phone. Only a couple of miles. No great thing," Turtle grated out in that marvelous-to-hear, indescribable broken voice of his.

A flood of memories, held back because up to now I had carefully avoided associations that would remind me of those times, came charging back. But this time I controlled myself.

"Hey, Bit, y'ain't waiting on me!" Turtle bellowed, batting halfheartedly at my hands as I unlaced his boots. I knew, despite his show of embarrassment, he was pleased. I'd done it before.

"And why not? Your fingers are too cold to do it and if you don't get these wet things off, you'll get pee-new-monia."

"Me!" roared Turtle indignant at the mere suggestion of such frailty. "Not on your life."

"Sergeant!" The major's voice crackled.

"Leave him be." I grinned up at Turtle "The sergeant's not himself without four-letter words. However, to ease your guardian conscience, the one and only time I mimicked him, he soaped my mouth out with army issue." I shuddered at the memory of that taste.

"That's right, Major, begging your pardon," Turtle put in, mindful that the major's one word had been tantamount to a direct order.

"At ease," the major said, mollified.

I bridled at such offhanded assumption of complete authority over my Turtle Bailey. United States Army notwithstanding, my claim on Turtle predated the major's. Turtle grinned at my bristling defense and laid a soothing hand on my shoulder. Another thought struck me and I stared at Turtle torn between surprise and irritation.

"Turtle, why in God's green world didn't you tell Major Laird that James Carlysle Murdock is a girl?"

"Huh?" Turtle was so astonished I knew he couldn't be acting. I'd seen him pull incredible performances on visiting generals and colonel's wives. But he was not shamming now. "Didn't he know?"

I rocked back on my heels as the second boot suddenly released its watery grip on Turtle's foot.

"No, he didn't," I said with a sideways glance at the major as I propped up the soaking footgear by the fireplace.

"Bailey didn't know your father had appointed me your guardian either," Laird put in, absolving Turtle of all guilt. It also left me unable to pass the buck. "I was wounded not long after your father . . . died, you know. Between his death and the push towards Julich, there wasn't much time for talk."

It was then I noticed the purple heart bar among the stuff

44

on Turtle's barrel chest. I stared, grabbing the sergeant's arm, and pointed to it.

"Turtle where?" I gasped.

"Huh? Aw, knock it off, Bit," Turtle growled. "I only took it fer points. I wanted out."

I shook his arm because I didn't believe for a moment that was the reason. It was then I began to wonder. What on earth was Turtle doing looking up a major on a stormy day at the elbow of Cape Cod? Furthermore they were both looking awfully ill at ease. Which had nothing to do with a silly girl's tears. They were hiding something from me. In that moment I began to feel the first tendrils of an honest fear. Merlin picked up my embryonic apprehension and growled softly in his throat. He's uncanny in his ability to sense mood shifts and not just in me. His soft growl intensified my uneasiness. The dog and I exchanged glances just as the major and Turtle did.

"I didn't know you'd copped it," Laird remarked. He proffered cigarettes but Turtle shook his head, reaching into his breast pocket for the ghastly Fatimas he preferred. His battered face broke into a grin as he pointed to his ear. I saw then that the tip of his ear was missing as well as the first joint of his index finger on the left hand, the stump barely healed.

"Goddamnedest fool _____ piece of luck. We mopped up at Julich after you got hit, Major. Then hooked up with the Hundred and Sixteenth because the krauts had shot the hell out of the unit in those _____ _____ _____ beetflelds. You know some rear echelon fart named Warren, a light colonel, after you got clobbered?"

The major nodded solemnly, his jaw muscles working.

"Jeeze, Bit, I thought the general had that _____ pegged for what he was," Turtle hissed at me through his teeth. "_____ rear echelon—"

"Knock it off!" the major ordered curtly, his eyes flashing.

Turtle was not going to be intimidated by any rank lower than four stars and he was only polite then.

"Wal," he continued blandly, "we were knocking the _____ out of a block in Julich. Snipers on the roof, in the cellar, you know the drill. I was waving the squad up," he demonstrated, "when some _____ sniper winged me. Got the BAR man behind me though, right through the eye."

"You mean, you . . ." I gasped, utterly unable to believe the indestructible Bailey pulled a blighty for an earlobe and a finger joint.

"_____ no!" Turtle exploded indignantly. "I didn't even report it till I got the major's letter. Then I hunted up the medic and took my points."

"What letter?" I asked suspiciously.

"The letter that the major was invalided stateside." Turtle was evading now and he knew I knew it even if the major didn't.

Obviously I wouldn't get Turtle to come clean with the major hanging on every word. Whatever was going on between those two did concern me. Of that much I was sure. How, why, I hadn't an inkling but I wasn't going to leave this house until I found out. I had the feeling it also concerned Dad. But, if Dad were involved and he had never been anything but a good soldier, why wouldn't Turtle level with me? Unless, of course, the major had antiquated ideas about helpless females or me blabbing about company business.

"Well," I said rising abruptly, "with *two* guardians, one of them totally above reproach, I can stay on here."

"No!" they chorused explosively.

"Now you two knock it off. I don't know what gives between you but I want you to know, you're not fooling me for one split second."

"This isn't a woman's concern," Laird answered hotly, the ridges of his scars reddening.

"Women. Ha! Have you men done so well with the world?" I asked with fine scorn. I turned on Turtle who had the grace to look abashed. "I'll bet *you* never even stopped to eat in town," I accused him. Turtle shook his head in quick affirmation.

"Well, I'll fix you something to eat," I offered grudgingly.

"Get some clean socks from the major. You both appear to wear the same size shoe when your feet aren't in your mouths." I flounced out of the room, slamming the door with a satisfactorily resounding crash.

I'd get it out of Turtle in my own way and the hell with the major. I poked unnecessary wood in the range, burning my finger on the hot plate-iron top. With more caution, I pulled the coffeepot onto a front ring and hunted in the icebox for the Dutch kettle. I knew we hadn't consumed all the stew last night. Turtle was very partial to stew. The idea of Turtle trying to put one over on me, I muttered to myself.

The stew was not, absolutely not, in the refrigerator. Congealed messes, improperly covered, and some partially molded over, two bunches of good carrots and four limp stalks of celery, a half-gallon metal can of milk almost full, a huge wheel of butter, a bowl of eggs, a slab of bacon, and an indecent quantity of beer completed the inventory of the box, but no stew.

"If I were stew, where would I go?" I asked myself a la Stanislavsky.

Merlin whined at the back porch door. I guessed that the men had let him out the study door. Exasperated, I let him in.

Now I can't say he overheard me muttering, but as I opened the door I caught sight of the iron kettle perched on the shelving on the back porch. I peered inside and the contents were frozen solid. Naturally, important things like beer should be kept at a proper degree of refrigeration, I muttered to myself, whereas relatively unimportant items like a meat stew, not to mention the chickens I had also observed in cold storage and the hunk of meat, would be left to their own devices against the weather. First things first.

By the time I had washed up the backlog of dishes, the stew had thawed and was simmering. There was more than enough for all three of us to eat our fill. The major's culinary skill seemed limited to making up quantities of one thing that would last for days. That might be all right for him, himself alone, but not this li'l chile.

47

I gave a chow yell and heard Turtle hop to with a "Yo." He padded down the corridor in, I hoped, fresh-stockinged feet. I heard his oath as the steaming hot water in the bathroom sink caught him by surprise.

When he and the major entered the kitchen, they both had that look about them which meant they'd confirmed their idiotic boy scout pact. They made a determined effort to forestall any reopening of the subject while I was equally determined to ignore the whole ploy.

I served Turtle first, grinning at the gusto with which he attacked the meal.

"Major," he said around a generous mouthful of meat and potato, "you make the best goddam stew this side of the Divide. That includes . . . hmmmmah . . . all Europe." He pointed his fork at me, waving the potato speared on it like a baton. "Bit, you shoulda tasted the rabbit stew the major scrounged up near Montcornet." (He mutilated the French pronunciation.) "Jeezuz but that tasted good." He smacked his lips retrospectively. "Marty got the rabbit. Big bastards over there, they are."

"Was it Landrel or the Bum who liberated the vegetables?" the major asked, grinning.

"The Bum," and the curt way Turtle answered indicated both men were now dead.

"That one could scrounge from St. Peter," was the major's admiring accolade. Turtle nodded his head, his mouth too full to speak.

"Bosworth swapped K rations for some vin ordinaire as I recall," and there was nothing wrong with the major's accent. Regan Laird took up the tale, "and M. LeMaitre loaned us a pot . . . against his wife's better judgement."

Gravy spilled out of the corners of Turtle's mouth as he grinned at the memory. He caught the gravy deftly with a hunk of bread, then popped bread and all in his mouth, licking his fingers.

"And then," Turtle shook with malicious mirth, "the mutts in the village cornered Warren and he never did get anything to eat. Then he tried to get the colonel to give us hell because we weren't supposed to be bivouacking in the village, annoying," Turtle snorted with contempt, "annoying the inhabitants. Annoying? Hell, they adopted us!"

Mention of Warren was sobering. It improved my opinion of the major that he shared our dislike of Major . . . no, damn it, Colonel Donald Warren.

I had always hated Warren myself. No one ever succeeded in convincing me that he hadn't poisoned Merlin's litter brothers. He was irrationally frightened of dogs, any dog, down to and including a Chihuahua. And I knew for certain he had been instrumental in putting away Morgan le Fay, Merlin's dam. Warren could swear and allege all he wanted to but I'd never believed Morgan had bitten him. She had more sense. She'd've got blood poisoning. Dad had been off post at the time and, because Marian Warren was toadying up to the C.O.'s wife, neither Turtle, I, nor the Downingtons, who owned Morgan, could change the edict.

It infuriated me that Warren had assumed Dad's command, however briefly, after Major Laird had been wounded. It was intolerably bitter to me that Donald Warren still walked the earth and my father was under it. War is not only hell, it is too damned indiscriminate in its victims.

"I always wanted to know, Bailey," the major was saying, his eyes twinkling, "if you and Casey had anything to do with the bedroll problem?"

"Bedroll. . . ." Turtle was seized with a violent paroxysm of choking, complicated by a fit of laughter that brought tears to his eyes.

"Bedroll?" I asked suspiciously.

Regan Laird's grin threatened to break open scar tissue. Chuckling, he managed to explain.

"Ah, Major Warren seemed to have trouble keeping his bedroll free of . . . ah . . ."

"Messages?" I cried, delighted.

"Messages," Laird agreed. That set Turtle off again so I had to pound his shoulder blades before he choked to an untimely end. Laird managed to straighten his face before he continued. "DeLord was of the opinion the dogs homed in on him. That right, Bailey?"

Turtle choked again, turning bright red, and this time Major Laird swatted him smartly on the back. Turtle finally got his breath back, downing a full can of beer to set things right.

"That . . . DeLord," he gasped finally, belching noisily. "'Scuse it. That DeLord! I can't figure him."

"Why not? Damn good officer. Thought on his feet."

"Yeah. Well, guess who got mighty thick with Warren after you got clobbered?"

"Not DeLord?" The major frowned in surprise.

"Yeah, DeLord," Turtle confirmed sourly. "I never figgered he'd suck up to Warren after the colonel was . . . buried."

Turtle looked stricken. He swallowed furiously, glancing nervously at the major. The major stared back at him angrily, his eyes snapping, and awkward silence settled on the room. I still wasn't up to discussing Dad's death, particularly with Turtle. And obviously the subject was as painful to the sergeant as it was to me.

"Is that . . . Dad's footlocker upstairs?" I asked.

Both men turned sharply around to glare at me. The major recovered first.

"Yes it is, Carlysle," he said quietly. "I spotted it at Division HQ and had it sent on with mine. Some idiot painted my name over it. The key should have been sent back with the other personal effects."

"Yes. I have it with me," I admitted before I realized this was exactly the information he wanted.

"You'll want to go through it, to make sure everything's accounted for."

"Yes, I will. When it warms up upstairs."

"Sure," the major agreed easily. I didn't miss the looks they exchanged as I rose to clear the dishes.

"I need some sacktime, Major," Turtle announced, kicking back his chair. He caught it with an experienced hand before it clattered to the floor.

"Colder'n a . . . cold upstairs," the major corrected himself.

"Oh, Turtle can use my room for a while," I suggested. "It's warm in there and this kitchen is a positive disgrace . . . even for a KP-less major."

"Good," exclaimed the major, rising purposefully. "I'll build a fire now in the back bedroom. Take the chill off."

They stomped away, glad to be out of my company. Merlin trotted off with them, infected by my irritation with the male sex. He gave me a backward look, chastened and reproachful. I didn't call him back but I wasn't angry with him.

4

MY SCOTCH FORBEARS would have regarded my day's work with as much satisfaction as I did. I literally peeled accumulated scum off cabinets, walls, floors, pots, pans, cans, bottles, glasses. I cursed unknown predecessors for slovenly habits even as I ignored the plain fact that probably the house had been untenanted for several years. I knew that Regan Laird had not been back from Europe for very long but even he must have been aware the kitchen was incredibly dirty.

Mother Bailey, Turtle's mother, had always scrubbed, caroling a lusty revival hymn in time with her strokes. It had been part of her philosophy that singing hymns was prayerful and being prayerful made work go faster, combining two virtues at one and the same time, rewarding doubly. I had spent two years with her in West Roxbury just after Mother's death, until I was school age. I know those few years were my happiest although I missed Dad sorely. However, I had uncles and aunts and cousins and grandparents galore. Ma Bailey's favorite for floor scrubbing was "Rock of Ages" which could set the crockery rattling as her volume increased in direct proportion to the amount of mud and dirt on the floor. She had a fine resonant contralto and her one criticism of her religion was that the Catholics had few decent "tunes" for scrubbing. As a matter of fact, she confided in me shortly after I came to her that she had felt it on her conscience to be singing Protestant hymns and had taken the Matter up with her parish priest. Looking back, I can see the humor of the situation and wonder how the priest had managed to control his mirth at such a question. Ma Bailey did receive the dispensation although she was scrupulous about choosing "nondenominational" anthems and avoiding any which mentioned the Trinity or the Virgin Mary. I might have turned Catholic in that household had I not heard how Turtle got his voice. Or rather, got the one he now used.

Despite all latrine gossip to the contrary, Master Sergeant

Edward Bailey's voice was not the product of years of parade ground drilling nor was his undamnable flow of blasphemy the result of frustration with "stupid squads." Born in Boston just before the turn of the century, of poor but honest folk, young Edward Bailey had been a handsome lad, a devout Catholic and, as soon as he was old enough, an altar boy. The parish priest had noticed the lovely quality of young Ed's voice in the repetition of the responses. It became apparent by the time he was ten that he was possessed of a naturally sweet, true soprano. He was quickly exploited and became known throughout the Boston metropolitan area, singing at high masses, weddings, funerals, association meetings, and such, billed as Boston's McCormack, a true Irishman. A brilliant career was projected for him, including entrance to a fine Catholic high school and college.

One evening, on his way home from a music lesson, a bunch of roughs, out on the prowl for any Irishman they could "put in his place" (for those were the days of the terrible Irish pogroms in Boston) attacked him, beating him so severely about the face and throat that his voice box was smashed and his face so brutally mutilated he bore no resemblance to the old tintype his mother cherished of her Eddie.

For months after the incident he could barely talk. But his early vocal training gave him one advantage, he could force air from his diaphragm for a semblance of speech. Gradually he was able to use his vocal cords again but the glorious voice was gone. The Church, without noticeable regret, canceled the scholarships. At sixteen, a battered-faced, embittered boy had lied about his age and enlisted in time to fight in the first World War. He had wanted to die but fate had assigned him to my father's first command. A comradeship was established at that Plattsburg training camp which had lasted my father's lifetime and seemed to spill over to include me.

Child though I was when I heard that story, I knew who had hurt my Turtle Bailey the most and the Catholics lost me. Turtle was even then my special haven. As a matter of fact, I was responsible for the nickname. Somewhere, somewhen, a biblical phrase had been repeated in my hearing, the one about "and lo, the voice of the turtle was heard in the land." I'm told that I asked Sergeant Bailey if he had a turtle's voice and once the notion stuck in my mind, I never got rid of it.

Ma Bailey always claimed that one of the fringe benefits of floor scrubbing was solving problems. It only solved one of mine today, cleaning the floor. But I did cast the problems up and down, around and sideways, which could be considered the first step towards solving them. If you happened to be of an optimistic nature.

My first problem was staying on in this house. Then finding out what was going on between the major and the sergeant. Did it have to do with my father? And why? Did it have something to with the burglar? The footlocker?

The floor was drying. The walls and cabinets were sparklingly clean and everything within them. The rest of the house was too cold to assault with mop and pail except for the bathroom. So I launched a major offensive against it, whipping it into a sanitary state in next to no time. I came back to the nice clean kitchen and slumped down in a chair, to revive myself with coffee and mull over dinner. In Ma Bailey's lexicon, cleanliness was next to godliness but food was what a man wanted next to him. At least, that was the version I learned at six.

I brought the chickens in from the back porch, the poor things. I must tell the major, war or not, he was not to patronize again whoever sold him those birds. They'd obviously been running around since the last war. The only decent thing to be done with them was stew. As I recalled it, Turtle was partial to my dumplings. At the moment I had no desire to satisfy my guardian's preferences. Then, too, there was nothing like a full stomach to tempt a man to lose his discretion.

My years of boardinghouse living had had several hazards. One was that if the proprietress was widowed or single, she made a play for my father. This usually began with intense concern for the well-being of his daughter, with much discussion about my lack of feminine skills such as housekeeping, cooking, and sewing. I don't know whether I learned to cook in my self-defense or Father's but I also don't remember not knowing how to cook. Once each new aspirant discovered me versed in fundamentals, she would undertake to instruct me in fine points so I had acquired culinary arts above the ordinary. In fact, I earned all my spending money now cooking, with two regular dinner jobs a week and two lunchtime positions.

Even my skill was challenged by these fowl. Fortunately the larder was not bare of herbs, in fact, the inventory was extraordinary. The inequalities included five half-used boxes of paprika, nine thyme, three rosemary, but no marjoram. Lots of oregano, but no basil. Still I had enough of the right things. It looked to me as if the summer renters had always brought their own spices and then left them behind in the hectic windup of seasonal withdrawal.

I made a cake, reveling in the unusual amount of honest-to-gosh butter. As I slid the cake pans into the oven, I realized there was no heat gauge. The oversupply of wood I had petulantly rammed in had burned off and the oven innards did not seem over hot on my skin. If Grandma could do it, I could!

The cake rose and rose, unevenly to be sure, but it was a home-baked product and they could like it or lump it. I heard stamping on the back porch and when I peered out of the crystal-clear window, the major glanced at me questioningly. When I smiled, he pointed to the woodbox. I shook my head. He loaded up and I heard him crashing back in again, slamming the door to his study. Then the kitchen door opened.

"Have you . . . hey, what happened to the kitchen?" he asked, coming all the way in and looking around with a pleased smile.

"Where's your white glove?"

His grin broadened. "No need. I appreciate this, I really do. I've been trying to get a woman out here but no luck." He opened a cabinet and peered in. He whistled, his fingers absently stroking the now greaseless wood.

I held the coffeepot aloft suggestively. Just then he spotted the cake cooling on the table. There was a curious look on his face as he reached mechanically for a cup.

"Maybe I'm glad you're not James Carlysle," he said, looking down at me as I poured his coffee. A shadow of an odd expression flitted across his face.

"Oh, I've been promoted to human status?" I asked.

He lifted his mug in a toast. The lid of the Dutch kettle rattled, drawing his eyes from mine to the stove. He took a deep sniff.

"That mouth-watering aroma cannot possibly come from those desiccated carcasses in the hall?" he inquired.

I shrugged nonchalantly. "Naturally. Even retreads from the last war cannot daunt Chef Murdock."

He winced. "I know what you mean. And, at that, the farmer assured me it was a favor from one vet to another."

"Favors like that you don't need! Particularly in wartime."

He tilted the lid, breathing deeply.

"Ambrosial! You put my efforts to shame."

"You've merely lacked the touch of a woman about the house."

He straightened quickly, his face cold.

"I wouldn't be too sure of that," he said in a flat voice and turning on his heel went directly back to his study.

I stared after him, curiously sensitive to his rebuff. He hadn't mentioned a wife and he wore no ring. If he were married, it wouldn't have bothered him that I was unchaperoned. Surely he'd want his wife with him right now, or maybe he wouldn't with his face like that. No, I couldn't buy that theory. You don't marry a guy just for his good looks. Can that, too, Carla. You know damned well some girls have married guys for the set of their shoulders in a military tunic.

I iced the cake unenthusiastically, the edge of my pleasure blunted by the incident. I regarded the respectable product of my labors with a jaundiced eye and put it on the sideboard. I tasted the stew and salted it again. After I had peeled carrots and potatoes and added them, I set the table for dinner.

The kitchen clock said six although it felt earlier. Because, I supposed, the day had begun late. I peeked out into the hall and noticed my other bag. The side pocket of the B-29 canvas bag bulged with the box of Dad's personal effects. That reminded me that the key to the footlocker was at hand and the footlocker above my head in the back room.

Well, I might as well clean up that detail. If the inventory of my father's effects was going to reduce me to tears, at least there were sympathetic shoulders at hand. And I might just find out what it was the major thought I'd find in that locker.

By the time I had wrestled the bomber bag up the stairs, the chill of the house had taken away the heat of my desire to circumvent the major. I really didn't want to look through that locker. For that matter, I hadn't even looked very carefully past the first layer of the box. The sight of Dad's West Point ring, tied to the end of the liberty scarf he'd bought me in England, had been too much for me. I had shoved the Vmail letters and the photo case that formed the first layer over the scarf and closed the box. I hadn't been able to open it up again.

Irresolute, I stared at the door to the back room. The stamp albums must be in the footlocker; the box was too small for them. And the stamps were valuable. I wasn't the philatelist my father had been but I'd learned enough about stamps so that I wouldn't be cheated much if I were forced to sell the collection. Stamps didn't depreciate and if diamonds were a girl's best friends, stamps were a man's . . . or a refugee's. He'd mentioned picking up some surcharged Polish stamps and three French Colonial oddities in Paris the one time he'd had leave there. I'd better ask the major if the stamps oughtn't to be evaluated. Wartime or not, there were certain formalities for a hero's heir.

Come to think of it, Dad had mentioned that this DeLord had been with him on that Parisian foray. Dad's opinion of DeLord had been favorable and Dad was an infallible judge of men. Why were the major and Turtle contemptuous of the lieutenant? Of course, if the man were so ill-advised as to consort with Warren, I could understand their dislike. But, if Dad had liked DeLord, why was DeLord cozying up to Warren? Oh, it made no sense. Irritated by my indecision, I kicked the bomber bag against the wall. It could stay there. It was too cold to go through Dad's things. Even basically impersonal things such as stamps. I turned on my heel and went to my own room.

I knocked. I banged. I pounded. Well, Turtle always could sleep up a storm when he put his mind to it. I opened the door, closing it quickly because the room was warmer by noticeable degrees than the hall.

Turtle was snortingly asleep, a quilt half covering his husky frame. He was lying on his back, his head to one side, one hand across his chest, the other tucked under the pillow. Never a lovely sight, with his broken thick nose, the heavy, undershot jaw, the pitted scarred face with its shadow of new beard growth, he made Lon Chaney look like Robert Taylor by comparison. With the familiarity of our friendship, I marched up to the bed and shook him by the shoulder. The next thing I knew, a Luger was pressed to my temple and a beefy hand was tight on my throat.

"For Pete's sweet suffering sake," I managed to say in a normal voice although I was never more startled in my life. Had I struggled or screamed, I think I might have been killed.

"Chrissake, Carla," Turtle exploded in an angry roar of relief, "never do that to a combat fighter. I'd've blown your brains out. Chrisssst!" and he snapped the safety on and flopped back onto the bed, as shaken as I by the incident.

I sat down limply on the foot of the bed, rubbing my throat.

"I knocked," I explained plaintively. "Then I banged and I pounded, Turtle."

He nodded understandingly. "I'm too used to sleeping through barrages, Bit." He rubbed the back of his neck and jerked his head around sharply so that something cracked hollowly. This made him feel better but it made me nervous. "Best thing to do is call me by name."

"Sergeant? Or," and I grinned maliciously, Turtle?"

His glower dissolved into an affectionate grin.

"Sarge," he suggested with a gravelly growl. He raised himself up, deftly knocking a single cigarette from the pack to his lips. "Jeez but it's good to see you, Little Bit. You're as thin as a stick but you look great to this old horse."

"It's wonderful to see you, too," I agreed, "but I don't exack-a-tally like you hobnobbing with the brass before coming to see me."

Turtle scowled, his glance sliding from mine before he looked back. "I did. I called your boardinghouse and you'd gone out somewhere."

"When?" I exclaimed, annoyed I hadn't been told of his call and sick I hadn't seen him earlier.

"Day before yesterday. I'd just got in."

"Day before . . . Oh, yes. Mrs. Everett did say I'd had a couple of phone calls. I was at the dean's," and I grimaced at the memory of that "take-it-easy-now" interview. "You called twice."

"Naw," he contradicted, surprised. "Just once. Like I said. The, lady didn't know when you'd be back. And I got . . . involved."

I grinned at him and he waved off the suggestion in my smile that he'd gone off on a bat.

"When I called yesterday morning, you'd just left for the major's. So I came on down. Lined up my targets."

"Why did you have to see the major?" I asked as casually as I could.

Turtle looked at me squarely in the face, his jaw set, his eyes bleak.

"Comp'ny business," he growled in a flat no-nonsense voice.

"One of my father's companies?" I asked.

Turtle didn't so much as blink.

"I've known you since you were an hour old, James Carlysle Murdock. This is company business and that's all you'll get from me. Flat out!"

There is nothing stubborner than a Boston Irishman when he gets set. I'd seen Turtle like this a couple of times before.

Once with an inspecting general and it wasn't Turtle who gave in. I acknowledged his obstinacy by standing up abruptly.

"Made you chicken 'n' dumplings. And the sun's over the yardarm."

Turtle's face broke into a slow, grateful smile. He cuffed me affectionately on the shoulder. "Good girl."

He rose and said, through a massive yawn, "Sprung a bottle loose from my sister's bastard of a bartending husband. God, but he's stingy."

"She must like him. She married him."

"Ha! Don't remember Rend very well do you? She had to!" Turtle's mirthless laugh was accompanied by the multiple crackling of his knuckles.

"Oh, you know I hate that sound, Turtle. Speaking of marriage, is the major?"

Turtle looked at me sharply.

"Or is that company business too?" I added sweetly.

Turtle shook his head. "He was married." The sergeant paused thoughtfully. "But it broke up sometime before Pearl. He's been in a while but he's no Pointer."

His bachelor status was more of a relief to me than it should have been, considering our brief association. His not being an Academy man was a surprise. I could usually spot the ninety-day wonders. The way Turtle looked at me then decided me against further pumping. It was natural for me to want to know the scuttlebutt about my guardian but if Turtle was reticent about the major, there was no surer indication of the old sergeant's respect for him.

"Major well liked?"

Turtle nodded solemnly and I left it at that. As Turtle rummaged in his bag for the bottle, I closed the door quietly. I got the locker key from my B-29 and turned resolutely to the back room. If they won't tell me, I'll find out myself.

An old chest of drawers had been pushed next to the three footlockers. So, with some pushing and shoving, I got the top locker onto the chest. The major was probably in his study so he wouldn't hear me rumbling things.

The key fit into the lock all right enough but it took me a little time to get the key to turn the tumblers. Salt air probably, plus the freezing temperatures of the room.

Gritting my teeth, I threw the lid up, exposing the compartmented tray on top. I sighed deeply; there certainly wasn't much to cry about in this assortment of badly mimeographed orders of the day, manuals, language dictionaries, torn map fragments, handkerchiefs and unmatched socks, thready shoulder patches. I could even regard Dad's Sam Browne belt sanguinely. I poked around unenthusiastically until I realized I was evading the issue.

I lifted the tray out and below it were things that had meaning for me. Stolidly I lifted out the top stamp album. It was, naturally, the very one I'd given him for Christmas three years ago. I found myself stroking the red leather, tracing the gold tooling with an idiot finger as my throat began to tighten. I shook my head, resolved not to cry again, and leafed carefully through the pages. These were his commemoratives and consequently incomplete. I put it carefully aside, my fingers trembling as I reached for the two blue albums, recalling how often they had appeared on the evenings which Dad and I had spent companionably together. He'd spread them out on a table or the bed, losing himself in his hobby for hours of patient study and arrangement, cursing because he missed the one vital stamp that would double the worth of the unit. Beneath the two blue books was the shabby brown one which had been his first. I lifted it a few inches and then dropped it hurriedly. For it covered the triangular shape of a folded flag and that was too much.

Hastily I put the other three album backs in place and started to unpack the other end of the locker. A canvas wrapped rectangle disclosed a handsome, blue leather, goldtooled volume bearing the inscription "Briefmarken." This must have been the German album he had picked up in Paris which had excited him so much. I opened it and two pieces of foolscap fell out. In Dad's handwriting at the top of the first sheet was the initial "D." D for Dad? Dog Company?

Below was a list headed "French China," broken into several categories. The first was headed "hand stamped," carmine and purple, 1903, 1900, 1902-4. The second included stamps from 1 centime to 75, with the 75 underscored heavily to Tchongking, Mong-tseu, Yunnan Sen (Yunnanfu) also Packhoi.

I dredged up what I could remember of half-heard philately lectures from Dad. The 75-centimes was something special but I couldn't remember what. I did remember that before the Boxer Rebellion in 1900 many of the foreign countries involved in that blatant exploitation had maintained their own postal offices, quite rightly distrusting the vagaries of the Chinese system. Had Dad actually run across a complete series? Oh, that would be a find. I leafed through the album carefully. There were even some of the 75-centimes stamps from each of the various French-China offices, a rather odd combination of deep violet and orange.

I looked back at the list. Just before the carmine and purple handstamp on the 1900 category and the 75-centimes in all the French-China divisions was a tiny check mark. I glanced again into the album but the ones checked were there. Well, I'd have to dig out the Scott Stamp Catalogue and see what exactly he meant. Perhaps these were more valuable. Although even as it stood these particular stamps were valuable by themselves if I remembered correctly.

Beneath the Briefmarken volume were two more rectangular shapes, carefully wrapped in heavy paper, neatly tied with thin cord. I felt the edges, assuming these were more albums; evidently the covers were made of wood. Or these might be the little surprise Dad had bought and never had time to mail to me. Well, I couldn't look at them right now. I pushed them to one side and there, half hidden by underwear and socks, were several boxes of forty-five shells and Dad's service revolver, holster and all. Turtle was slipping up badly, sending live ammunition and a gun. I'd roast him for it.

I grabbed up the gun, replaced the albums and the tray, and closed and locked the trunk. I eased the top locker back into place, more because I was used to putting everything back the way I'd found it than because I wished to hide the fact I'd been inspecting it.

I was halfway across the dining room when I heard Turtle roaring in a voice that could have penetrated armor plate. "Proof? Christ, what d'ya need proof for? Who else could have done it?"

"Proof to stand up in a court-martial, damn it, Bailey," I heard the major's equally incensed voice reply. Outside the house, Merlin barked, a sharp punctuation to their dispute.

"You can't be judge, jury, and executioner, Bailey," the major continued urgently. "And don't try it again."

Merlin barked again and I heard someone let him in. Then he scratched at the corridor door in front of me, sensing my presence even if the men did not.

"Major, if you think I'm going to let that murdering . . ."

"Can it, Bailey," Regan Laird warned curtly. Before I could move, he had jerked the door open. Merlin, delighted, wove around me, crooning, nosing my dangling hands. Regan Laird, his face stern, his eyes narrowing slightly, looked down at me accusingly. Wordlessly, he pushed the door wide for me to enter.

His face flushed with anger, Turtle was standing stolidly in the center of the room. Merlin circled me nervously, whining a demand for reassurance in the midst of the taut silence.

"Who's a murdering so-and-so, Turtle? What kind of proof do you need? For whose court-martial?"

Turtle's face closed down implacably.

"Where did you get that?" the major snapped, snagging the holstered revolver out of my hand. The cryptic conversation I'd overheard had put it out of my mind.

"From Dad's footlocker."

Turtle looked as if something had caught him a solid blow in the solar plexus. As the major drew the gun from its holster, Turtle poised as if he wanted to grab it out of the major's hands.

Laird broke open the gun. The cylinder was empty. He flipped the gun to the ceiling, squinting up the barrel. He and Turtle looked at each other over the weapon. They were both angry and disturbed.

"That's not my father's gun," I exclaimed, puzzled.

"No?" The major looked sharply at Turtle for confirmation. Reluctantly Turtle took the Colt, turning it in his hand to expose the handle.

"That isn't Dad's," I repeated, firmly. I knew the gun well, I'd cleaned it often enough, and the major's dubiety was irritating. "The right side of the handle was cracked. Here." I pointed out where the flaw should have been.

"She's right, all right, Major," Turtle stared at the gun as if it were evil. He dumped it back into the major's waiting hand as if he couldn't get rid of it soon enough. "Besides, I turned the colonel's Colt in to Ordnance before the corporal picked up his locker to take it back to Division." He stopped, his eyes widened, then he snapped his mouth shut.

Very slowly the major reholstered the gun as if he, too, found contact with it distasteful.

"If it isn't my father's gun, whose is it and why do you both act as if it were . . . poison or something?"

I glared at Turtle but he returned my stare, his eyes stubborn, his lips set in a thin line. I grabbed Laird's arm as he made to turn away.

"You've got to answer me. I demand to know!" I cried.

Laird looked down at me, the left side of his face towards me, his expression both pitying and angry.

"The gun is poison . . . if it's the one that killed your father."

5

"CHRIST, MAJOR," Turtle groaned in a hoarse voice, his face drained of all color, "she didn't have to know."

"I don't know what you mean," I said, dazed. I felt unreal. The words he had just said were not making any sense. My fathered murdered? He'd been killed. Killed! Not murdered!

The major put the gun on the mantelpiece before he looked at me again. When he did, his face hadn't changed. He had meant what he just said.

"No, Bailey, she should know because she'd find out anyhow." He sighed heavily. "Your father was killed by a forty-five slug."

"A forty-five slug?"

He nodded. I glanced, bewildered, at Turtle. Gray-faced, the sergeant confirmed it.

"No. No! No!" I cried, turning from both of them, hugging my arms to my sides. Merlin whined urgently and I thrust him away, whirling back to the men. "I just won't believe it. It doesn't make sense. I could see someone shooting Warren. God knows he was hated but not my father. Not Dad. The men loved him. He ran a good regiment. No one ever complained about Dad, did they, Turtle?"

Turtle nodded slowly.

"Maybe it was a sniper . . . got hold of a forty-five?" I suggested frantically. "It was a mistake? It wasn't murder!"

The major took me by the shoulders and gave me a hard shake; his eyes were compassionate but I hated him.

"No, Carlysle, it was no sniper. It could have been a mistake," he admitted slowly, heavily, as if he wished wholeheartedly he could accept that. "DeLord was driving your father to Warren. It was late. God knows . . . but Bailey and I now have reason to think it was murder."

"I don't understand," I cried, trying to twist away from the major, wanting to go to Turtle who stood so immovable, so silent, his stricken eyes dominating his white face. "I just don't understand."

My eyes lighted on the gun.

"Why did you say *that* gun killed my father?"

"I didn't. I said it might have. Now listen. to me. Your father was still alive when DeLord brought him in. We got the medic but there wasn't anything he could do. But a Colt, particularly at short range, makes a recognizable . . ." he broke off, struggling to make this horrible recitation easier on my feelings. "It was a forty-five, not a rifle, not a German handgun. After your father died . . . the slug proved it."

"Turtle, you *know* who killed Dad. Who was it?" I shrieked, struggling to break the major's grip.

"You're as trigger-happy as he is," the major bellowed, his eyes blazing, his hands like bruising iron grapples I couldn't shake. "Now you listen to me, Carlysle. I'm just as anxious as you two to get your father's killer but I'm not so much the fool as to take matters into my own hands. With a little patience, I can get the law to do it. That Colt may be all we need to do it legally, properly. War *doesn't* give license to settle private quarrels." He glared significantly at Turtle.

"Why not?" I cried, one part of me white-hot for vengeance, the other shocked at such hysteria. "Why didn't you settle things then and there, the night Dad was killed? Why wait four months? Why let the murderer get scot-free?"

Laird gave me another bone jolting shake.

"We had a war on!"

The cliche brought me up short. I hated it for one thing: It had been used as the excuse for so much inefficiency and stupidity. Right now it was so revoltingly trite it made me nauseous. Yet I knew what he actually meant by the phrase and I was too army to ignore the significance. Sensing the change in me, Laird let me go.

"Now, sit down. You, too, Bailey, and we'll attempt to talk about this sensibly. There've been quite enough half-ass actions and assumptions." The major pinned Bailey with a withering stare. He looked back at me and saw my rebellion getting a second wind and pointed peremptorily at the couch. "Sit!"

I did, holding myself stiffly erect, disdaining the cushions inches behind me. Merlin, deciding the crisis was over, curled around by my feet and lay down. The major waited pointedly until Turtle seated himself on the other end of the couch.

"Now, Carlysle—"

"Would you have told me straight out if I had been a boy?" I interrupted him bitterly.

"Yes," the major agreed. "That would have been necessary."

"But not necessary for a girl, huh?" I retorted sarcastically.

"Bit . . . ," Turtle pleaded, speaking for the first time.

I cut him off impatiently. "A girl may not avenge her father's murder—"

"There will be no *avenging*," the major snapped violently.

"It's an archaic distinction. He was my father, boy or girl. I'm not delicate, not sheltered, not stupid."

The major cocked an eyebrow at me. "Then shut up and listen," he suggested in a dangerously soft voice.

I shut my mouth and folded my arms across my chest, glaring at him.

"The night your father died, we were bivouacked just north of Siersdorf. Your father had set up his command post in a shack near a coal mine we'd cleaned out two days before. The regiment was spread out all over the area. I'd been sent up with some units to help the One Hundred and Sixteenth at Setterich. Now, Bailey says DeLord was with your father for about an hour. Then a call came in from Division for your father. DeLord was sent to get Warren—"

"What was the call about?" I demanded.

The major took a deep breath. "I don't know. Right now I want you to understand the events as we have pieced them together. DeLord was sent to get Warren. But your father changed his mind and had DeLord drive him."

I glanced at Turtle who usually knew all my father's business whether Dad intended him to or not. Turtle gave a negative shake of his head.

"The sergeant was called to check on the ammo and rations that had just come up. When he got back to the pest, how long, Bailey?" .

"Half hour maybe."

"When Bailey got back, your father was gone and so was his jeep and his usual driver was fast asleep."

The major paused. "I was on my way to report myself back from Setterich when DeLord came in with your father."

I tried to force the picture out of my mind, of Dad unconscious and dying.

"At first we assumed it was a sniper," the major was saying in a dull voice. "We'd had a. helluva time cleaning out some kraut positions, north of the mine. Two men in a jeep, late at night on a forest road."

My imagination drew another horrible picture . . . the jeep bucketing along the dark, shaded road, the sudden crack of a . . . I closed my eyes and leaned wearily into the pillows behind me.

"As I said, the medic noticed the kind of wound and . . . removed the slug. Turtle and I made him keep quiet. We checked every single side arm in the area within the next couple of hours. None had been fired that recently and none were missing.

"But that one," I began, pointing to the fireplace, "where did it come from?"

Laird shook his head, sighing.

"Someone stashed it away," Turtle growled. He emphasized "someone" just enough to make me certain he knew who "someone" was.

"Knock it off, Bailey,"

"Stashed it away," Turtle continued stubbornly, "so we wouldn't find it that night and then slipped it into the colonel's footlocker. Safest place in the world, you think about it."

"Ballistics can easily prove if that Colt killed your father," the major went on, ignoring Turtle's bitter aside. "The serial number will tell us who it was issued to. We go on from there."

Turtle snorted.

"Yeah, and suppose the Colt turns out to belong to some poor slob got killed back on the Cotentin," he sneered. "Where's your theory then? I tell you—"

"Bailey!" There was something about Regan Laird that daunted even Turtle. "That gun is important—"

"Fingerprints!" I cried out. "You smeared all the fingerprints just now."

The major dismissed that with an impatient wave of his hand.

"I am more interested in the two attempts made to break into your boardinghouse, Carlysle."

I stared at him blankly.

"Tell me, how long after your father's things arrived was the first attempt?"

"Just a day or two," I said, startled. "But I just had the box. And I only found the gun in the locker, today."

"Eyah," agreed the major pointedly, "but the thief didn't know the locker was delivered here."

"Chrissake!" Turtle exclaimed, scowling. "Colonel died in November. This is March. Took long enough."

"Oh, that's ridiculous. Why would the burglar—"

"If that gun does identify the murderer . . . If he did put it among your father's things as the safest place to hide it . . ."

"Look, Major, I packed the colonel's things myself. . . ."

"It's there now and as I remember it, we had to leave the locker open until Division had gone through it."

"Then someone in Division could have put it in and it needn't be connected with my father at all," I remarked sourly.

"Then why the two attempts to break into your room? What else were they after?"

I shrugged, having no answer at all. I still didn't feel the incidents could be related. There wasn't anything else of value in the locker or in the box. It would be a sophisticated burglar who wanted my father's stamp collection and he'd've had to know the stamps were in my possession.

"That doesn't answer why my father was murdered," I said finally into the silence of the room.

"No, it doesn't, and that is what has bothered me ever since it happened," the major said in a defeated voice. "It makes no sense. He was a damned good officer. Hell, he was wounded—"

"Wounded?" The word came out of me like a shriek. "Wounded?" I stared in horror at Turtle who flushed violently red. "Wounded! When?"

The major sat down, running his hand back through his hair. Elbows on his knees, he leaned forward to me.

"He'd got winged two days before, bullet grazed him in the ribs. He made the medic patch him and then pulled rank so it wouldn't be reported."

It was so like my father.

"Goddamned fool'd be alive today if he'd listened to reason," Turtle suddenly exploded, unleashing his accumulated tensions. "Chrissake, Gerhardt *knew*! Warren'd never got the regiment. Why'n hell did the colonel have to stay on the line?" Turtle hurled himself away towards the fireplace, futilely pounding at the heavy mantel. The gun bounced.

"Warren got the regiment? What d'you mean?"

The major shook his head from side to side, sighing again. "It's hard to piece this all together for someone who wasn't there. So much was happening so fast. That's why we made out it had been a sniper's bullet. The morale of the regiment was shot to hell after the beetfield massacre. . . ."

"Beetfields?"

"Look, let me explain and don't interrupt," and the major held up a cautionary hand. I nodded agreement.

"Our objective at the time was to join other elements of the Division for a major assault at Setterich. But we had to clear Siersdorf out beetfield by beetfield. We hadn't been warned there would be so much opposition. Company B and C were to advance. They hadn't got more than two hundred yards before the crossfire was murderous. Emsh . . . you remember Emsh?"

"Sure, who else ran Warren's company while Warren was sucking up to the C.O. of whatever post we were on?" I asked.

"Shut up. Emsh wanted to pull out and called back to the command post. Jim had gone up to see what was holding up the advance so Warren got on the walkie-talkie and started in on Emsh. Whatever was said, Emsh moved Charlie Company out again. They got pinned down in the rows of the beetfield. The krauts were taking a bead on the bulge of the combat packs.

DeLord ordered his company to shed theirs but he had to pull Baker back and Charlie was pinned flat. Your father got there and was grazed by a ricochet. By the time we mopped up the two German emplacements, there were only twenty men left of Charlie Company. Emsh was not one of them."

Turtle started swearing, softly, bitterly, accentuating each expletive with a dull thudding blow of his fist against the mantel until I was sure he'd bring his hand away bloody. He and Emsh had been boozing buddies; rivals in everything else. He would feel Emsh's loss as perhaps no one else ever could.

"Goddamned Warren killed him, that's what," Turtle said savagely.

"We had to wait for tank support to pulverize the krauts' positions before we could move up in that sector." The major winced, his face dark with suppressed anger. "That was another reason why Jim stayed on the line," he said.

"Gerhardt had rocks in his head. If only he'd known . . ." Turtle began.

"If he'd known, yes, but he didn't.'

"Known what?" I demanded of the major.

"Known your father was wounded. Instead he reamed him."

"Who? General Gerhardt? Reamed Dad? What for?"

"Failing to push on towards Setterich. Jim was told to quit fooling around, stop arguing about things . . . like beetfields . . . to quit stalling, pull up our socks, and get with it."

I stared at the major, incredulous at the general's reprimand. For one thing, my father was a helluva good line officer. The regiment had many citations. Surely the general must have known that my father's judgment was to be trusted.

"What the general didn't know was that not only was the colonel wounded, not that that mattered in the advance, but we hadn't enough officers. Captain Hainey was killed, Major Dunbar was badly wounded, and that left only Colonel Gregory, Major Sorowitz, me and —"

"Warren!" I inserted, beginning to understand. "So Father plays the hero because he won't let Warren get command of the regiment."

"Battalion," the major corrected me. "I was Exec."

"Why didn't Dad just transfer Warren back to Division HQ?"

The major shook his head impatiently.

"We didn't know, Carlysle. God knows, I suggested it, hinted at it, and when we moved into action at Baesweiler, I came right out with it. I told the colonel if he wanted the regiment to move out with any confidence, he'd better transfer Warren."

"And?"

The major grinned ruefully. Turtle looked disgusted.

"We got our heads handed to us," Turtle finally said.

"In no uncertain terms," the major said humorlessly, "we were told that Colonel Murdock still commanded the regiment. And until his command was challenged by the commanding general, he felt no need to explain decisions."

I blinked, visualizing the scene, picturing Dad's lean face, expressionless as he always was when agitated.

"His wound?" I asked tentatively, wishing to excuse my father's unusual autocracy.

Both the major and Turtle shook their heads slowly.

"Something was worrying him, Major," Turtle said slowly, frowning in concentration. "And I didn't have no clue. Not a one." Turtle's face reflected the hurt of this unusual reticence.

"He wouldn't have worried about turning the regiment over to you, Major," I remarked, "even with only a few officers."

"I think," the major began slowly, "it was more than relinquishing command just then . . . although the morale was pretty bad after the beetfield incident. Near as I can remember, the colonel started getting edgy around October."

"DeLord joined us in October," Turtle suggested.

The major shook his head violently. "DeLord's all right. I'd bet my bottom dollar on that."

"Dad liked him a lot."

"He sucked up to Warren when your dad was dead!" Turtle growled.

"C'mon Bailey, you must know what the colonel and DeLord were cooking up? They had too damned many quiet conferences."

Turtle glowered unhappily. "All I know is something about looting."

"If DeLord was the looter," I jumped on the idea, "and Dad was trying to make him make good, maybe DeLord killed him to keep HQ from finding out."

Both the major and Turtle dismissed that notion instantly.

"DeLord preferred a thirty-eight," Turtle said.

"And . . . he was . . . crying when he brought your father in," the major added softly.

The silence that followed those words was punctuated by the wind outside, by the spatter of snow driven against the windowpanes. It made no sense, Dad's Murder. Maybe it had been a mistake.

If Dad, after Donald Warren had goaded Emsh into disregarding his judgment about sending Charlie Company into the beetfield, had finally decided the man was too much of a menace in the regiment, had gone to order Warren back to the rear, why would Warren kill him? That was too straightforward an act for Donald Warren. His modus operandi would have been to slyly report my father's wounded condition to Division HQ and have Gerhardt order Dad relieved of duty. But Regan Laird would have assumed command, unless Warren tried to kill him, too, which made even less sense. For Warren, though he had never made any bones that he considered himself a superlative officer and a clever tactician, was not fond of the hazards of actual line duty. He didn't want to get killed. No, Warren would not have killed Dad to prevent his transfer.

Now possibly someone else, hearing Dad send DeLord for Warren, might have decided that the dark road was a good place to remove Warren permanently.

"How many were around when Dad sent DeLord for Warren?"

Turtle swivelled around, startled, his jaw dropping, his eyes blinking nervously.

"Huh? Half of headquarters company, but we all left to check the ammo and rations."

"Supposing," I suggested, hunching forward, "someone decided it was time to transfer Warren permanently?"

The major sighed. "I'd considered that as the strongest possibility until . . . Turtle found out about the looting."

"Looting?"

"Looting on an extensive scale."

"Yeah, Bit. The regiment was sometimes first into an area. Like the Cotentin lorry." He nodded to Major Laird who acknowledged the example. "A whole kraut truck trailer crowded with 'liberated' things. The CAO sent out directives every third day about what to look for in the kraut transports, stuff they'd made off with, what monuments not to bomb, that kind of crap. Kind of stuff your father detailed over to Warren to keep him out of the line. Only some of the stuff wasn't turning up at Division HQ."

"What does that have to do with Dad's . . . death?"

Turtle screwed his face up in thought. "I think the colonel got worried that someone in the regiment was holding back. One time I caught him planting some things on a bombed-out kraut truck near Baesweiler. Told me to forget what I saw and shut up." Turtle shrugged expressively.

I knew what he meant. Dad could be mighty short when he was worried and not even as long-standing an associate as Ed Bailey dared him in that mood.

"An officer?" I suggested, thinking of DeLord.

"Could have been anyone," Turtle replied. "Hell, all the guys swarmed over the stuff. We all lifted things here and there." He saw the major's glare and rose to the accusation blandly. "Sure, me too." Then his face hardened. "Until that _____ Warren started searching combat packs. Lousy _____!"

"Warren?" I asked, sitting up, my mind flipping through the possibilities. I might not feature Warren as a murderer but a thief? It was Regan Laird who pricked this theory.

"No, I saw the quantities of things the searches turned up. You could hide a piece here and there but not that much. Some of those wagon trailers had big canvases, heavy carved chests, old books," he explained. "Not stuff you could hide in a money belt or your shirt."

"Warren had a footlocker, didn't he?" I pursued.

Laird shook his head firmly. "Yes, but they don't hold much. And he'd have no way of getting loot back from the line. Does you no good to steal something you can't hide and can't send on. Beside, how would someone like Warren know what would be valuable?"

I gave a harsh laugh. "Same way the krauts would. And I suppose, if the krauts felt it worthwhile lifting from the French, it would be worth Warren's while, too."

"A point," Laird allowed but he was not convinced. He leaned forward, then, tapping me lightly on the shoulder. "Just remember, Carlysle, all this is only supposition. If it had been normal times, or even in an assembly area, we would have reported it to the MPs or the CID. But we couldn't." He glanced over my head to Turtle. "I know Bailey has it in for Warren but I'm afraid he's allowed other elements to cloud his judgment. Oh . . ." and he raised a hand to quell Turtle's resenting guttural, "that's one reason Turtle came down here, to enlist me in going after Warren and forcing a confession from him."

"But there's the gun now," I reminded him.

"Yes, there's the gun and there've been two attempts to burglarize your room. I'm asking why and although I can't figure out yet why someone would murder Jim Murdock, I can no longer believe it was a sniper. If there was widescale looting traced to our regiment, if Colonel Murdock knew about it and wanted to find the looter, that would account for him not wanting to leave the line for any reason. He had laid a trap . . ."

"Yeah, and he sent DeLord for Warren," Turtle reminded him.

". . . which would be an ample reason for Warren shooting father. . . ."

"But," the major interrupted us, "your father never got to Warren that night. He was killed on his way there."

"Then, if Warren isn't the looter, though I like that theory very much," I grinned wickedly, having many private reasons for hating Donald Warren, "whoever put that gun in my dad's locker knows it will connect him—Warren—with the murder."

"Exactly. But who's back?" the major asked sardonically. "I am. Turtle is . . ."

"DeLord's back and so is Warren," Turtle remarked in a very quiet voice.

"Warren?" I exclaimed.

"Yeah," and I have never seen such a horrible expression on Turtle's battered face. Involuntarily I drew back. "Yeah, Warren's back. He got wounded, you know, Bit," and the sergeant grinned knowingly at the major.

"Bailey?"

Turtle's eyes rounded with innocence. "He got hit at Aachen when we was clearing out each house in a block."

"Badly, I hope," I said vengefully.

"Smashed his shoulder real bad," Turtle replied, shaking his head ruefully.

"Not low enough, huh?"

"Carlysle!" Laird bellowed.

I grinned at him. "I have absolutely no use for Donald Warren."

"Neither do I but your indiscretion is inappropriate for a young girl—"

"But not a young boy?" I asked sweetly.

The major's eyes were snapping with anger and he was barely containing his own temper.

"All right, Bailey. I'm here, you're here, Warren's back, and so is DeLord. What we have to do is get that revolver out to Edwards and run a ballistics check—"

"When the storm settles down," Turtle interrupted.

The wind had indeed risen in volume and ferocity, as if stirred by the tenor of our arguments. Snow lashed at the windows, some particles sifting in around the old casements. Regan Laird turned towards the windows, listening to the storm's violence. His mouth curled in a faint smile as he realized the elements had abetted the sergeant's moratorium.

"That's a real cold sound, Major," Turtle said blandly.

I wondered if the major knew Ed Bailey as well as I did, because I knew that nothing was going to stop Turtle from killing Donald Warren. And I had no intention of apprizing the major of that knowledge.

Regan Laird looked speculatively at me. Abruptly I got to my feet, to break his train of thought lest I inadvertently betray myself.

"Good God, dinner!" I exclaimed with real feeling and dashed to the kitchen.

6

"SIR, SHALL WE break out the bottle?" I heard Turtle suggest as I left.

"Indeed!"

They followed me into the kitchen.

"Oh, man oh man, that smells like prime eating," Turtle ground out in a full bellow, rubbing his hands together in anticipation.

"Neat, water, or soda?" asked the major, getting out ice and glasses as I mixed dumplings.

"Neat . . . oh, that's when, sir. I want to taste that chicken."

"Soda for me," I put in.

The major hesitated briefly, the bottle poised over the glass. I saw Turtle's hamlike hand tilt the bottle generously into the glass. He gave it a courtesy dash of soda and some ice and handed it to me. Then his heels came together, his shoulders snapped back as he came to rigid attention, glass raised.

"The colonel . . . God bless him!" His voice made it more of a supplication than an invocation. I blinked the sudden tears from my eyes, raised the glass to touch theirs, and swallowed a stiff jolt.

"Did you hear what Timmerman said when he was told to cross that railway bridge at Remagen?" Turtle growled with suppressed amusement. He twisted a chair, its back towards the table, and seated himself, propping his heavy arms on the curved back of the chair.

The major, a smile twitching at the good side of his mouth, moved a chair catercorner from the table, stretching his long legs out just where I'd have to walk over them to get to the sink and back to the stove.

"Tell me," he urged.

I'm not sure it was Turtle's voice that made the story or Turtle's unusual vocabulary. Probably both plus the added fillip that both men knew the personalities involved and could enjoy an "inside" that I didn't have.

This Lieutenant Timmerman had discovered that although the railroad bridge at Remagen had been a target of the Allied air forces and had suffered some damage, it was back in commission. The Germans were flowing in retreat over it. When the enemy with their own curious logic decided the Americans would strike somewhere else, they withdrew the considerable strength at the Remagen bridgehead. Timmerman consequently found the bridge intact. Later that day the units supporting him controlled enough of the town to turn their attention to the bridge. The Germans were frantically preparing to blow it up. Timmerman was ordered to get across it before the Germans could succeed.

"And Major, get this. The lieutenant says to the general, 'What if the bridge blows up in my face?' Get it, blows up in my face? A lieutenant says that to a general! That's your new army for you," Turtle remarked with trenchant disapproval.

"Did it blow up?" I asked. After Dad's death I hadn't paid much attention to the First Army's advance.

"Naw, not then, It got shook up some, that's all. We crossed it. But I knew it wasn't the same army or the same war and I got out as soon as I could. Charlie Company was five men by the time we got to Coblenz. I'd had it."

I didn't for a minute doubt that once Turtle made up his mind to it, he could get sent home. He was such an old hand at red-tape cutting, I'm sure it was ostensibly legitimate. It just didn't sound like the Ed Bailey I knew.

I served their dinner and there was no more talk of war or any talk at all. Turtle paid me the compliment of eating with great concentration and gusto, passing his plate back three times. I had to whip up a second batch of dumplings as the major, though a more elegant trencherman, was equally hungry. Turtle's capacity had been a private joke for years but after three helpings of chicken 'n' dumplings, I hardly expected him to find room for three pieces of cake, too.

Merlin, who had napped on the far side of the stove while we were eating, woke. He stretched, walked majestically first to thrust his nose under Turtle's hand, then the major's, and then sat down expectantly by the kitchen door.

"Say, didn't he get volunteered for the K-9 Corps?" Turtle inquired, indicating Merlin with a cake-filled fork.

"He didn't make it," I grimaced, filling Merlin's bowl with what was left of the noontime stew.

"Naw!" Turtle's eyes went round with amazement. He hitched his chair around to get a full view of the shepherd. "You don't mean it. Him? I'd've though he'd be a good kraut killer."

"I did pull rank on them," I explained, "and made them give him an honorable discharge. But the fact remains he was considered of 'an insufficiently aggressive personality' for the Corps."

Turtle made a rude gesture. I giggled because the major glared so fiercely.

"If you were regular army," I told Laird, "you would know that army brats like me can't be shocked by mere sergeants."

"I don't get it," and Turtle shook his head sorrowfully, "he had half the rookies and two thirds of officers' row at Riley scared puking."

"Particularly Warren," I chortled nastily. "I swear, Turtle, he poisoned those other pups when he found out base families were going to take them. You know as well as I do that he made the Downingtons put Morgan away. She never bit him. She had more sense."

"Didn't I go to the C.O. myself?" demanded Turtle, his eyes wide at the implication he hadn't helped.

"That you did. Honest to God though, why couldn't it have been Warren who got killed?" I cried angrily. Turtle looked away.

"Any coffee?" the major asked, breaking the uncomfortable silence.

I slammed across the room for cups and back to the stove for the pot. The major's raised eyebrows cautioned me to get a hold of myself. I poured carefully.

"Warren's back, too, you said?"

"As a matter of fact," drawled Turtle, stirring spoonful after spoonful of sugar into his cup, "he came back on the same ship I did." He put his spoon very carefully down, right next to the knife he had not used. He straightened both so they were precisely aligned and then looked the major in the eye.

The major sipped his hot coffee, his eyes never leaving the sergeant's. His left eyebrow arched slightly.

"He joined his missus in Boston day before yesterday. I believe he planned to pay a courtesy call on Miss James Carlysle Murdock."

"Of all the insufferable, patronizing, condescending, ridiculous, hypocritical, vicious, egregious, inconsiderate, vile, contemptible, despicable. . . ." I sputtered, rigid with indignation, unable to categorize what I felt from my guts about Lieutenant Colonel Donald Warren.

"I think that's very interesting," the major remarked when I momentarily ran out of appropriate adjectives. He didn't, however, mean my descriptive venom. He meant that Warren was in Boston and proposing to call on me. "I'd very much like to know why he felt constrained to call on you."

That drew me up short for I had been about to launch into another tirade, having recovered my eloquence. I glanced at Turtle and then did a double take on him. The look on his face was a killing one, a hating one, far more expressive of what I felt for Warren than any word fashioned by man to express inner violences.

"You do think Warren killed my father, don't you Ed Bailey?"

Turtle's head turned sharply around to me and I saw the deadly hatred in his eyes, and something else, unfathomable and unfamiliar.

"He only thinks so," Major Laird interposed in a steely voice. "But I want to know why first. There is more to this whole goddamned mess than a fine man's death. I want to know what. Is that clear, Bailey?" The major spaced those last words out very carefully, as if cutting the orders of the day ineradicably on Turtle's consciousness.

Turtle swung his head slowly back to face the major.

"Yes sir," he grated out softly. "Very clear, sir."

Merlin, sensing the aura permeating the room, looked up from his dinner and growled deep in his throat.

7

THE DETAILS of living got us through the rest of the evening. I washed the dishes while the two men chopped wood and replenished the fireplaces and wood buckets throughout the house. Thanks to a fall survey course in English literature I cleverly thought of heating bricks to warm the beds.

The wind had risen higher with nightfall and the snow was swirling and howling around the Point where occasionally white-capped waves lunged to the top of the protective dunes. Within the house, despite its chilling discussions, there was warmth and companionship.

By the time the chores had been done and Merlin let out for a brief run, we were all ready to turn in for the night. Perhaps as much to be alone with our various thoughts as to sleep. Maybe the others felt, as I did, that all should sleep on what had been said and suspected.

My room was warm and the wrapped hot brick did take the clammy chill off the sheets. With Merlin stretched comfortingly beside me, I should have slept. I think I did but it was a restless slumber and shallow, for any crackling of the fire or sudden whine of the wind at the shutters roused me.

I was awake when I heard the minute clink of the latch moving on its tracks. Merlin raised his head briefly but his body did not tense. He didn't even mutter a growl. He put his head back down, sighed, and slept. I could feel the cold from the hallway and, through slitted eyes, I saw a figure cross the room. The dying fire lit the gargoyle side of the major's face as he softly stepped across the floor. He bent over the fire and quietly added more logs. He turned back, I closed my eyes tightly, then remembered to relax the muscles of my face. I could feel a difference in air pressure as he stood right by my bed. I could feel Merlin turn his head and I felt motion through Merlin's body against mine as the major scratched the shepherd's muzzle. Then lightly, so gently I couldn't be sure whether it was his fingers or just the air current preceding the withdrawal of his hand, I felt him touch my hair, much as I had his the previous night.

When he had left, I wondered if he were mocking me. Had he seen my eyes a trifle open? Had he been awake last night when I had caressed him in similar fashion? Caress, I suddenly admitted to myself, was the proper word. Because caress implies tenderness, affection, desire. I could chide myself all the way from Orleans to Boston on any cold, uncomfortable baggage car, yet not escape the fact that the major was more man than I had been next to in a long time and I was—to be blunt—man-hungry. These years when I should have been dating, dancing, having fun with boys were empty. The boys were embattled in far places. I remained in chaste loneliness. By virtue of a life as an army child, I understood the world of men better than most girls, but I understood it as a child and not as a woman. The major, wounded and embittered, was a magnificently romantic figure. This whole crazy situation of his being my guardian was romantic in the Gothic tradition. Ridiculous when my father must have known exactly . . .

My train of thought stopped with an icy jerk. The realization that my father had known exactly what he was doing in assigning me to Laird's guardianship dawned on me. He'd've known that the major's type was attractive to me. He'd had plenty of opportunity to judge what kind of man I liked, or what kind of man he'd prefer me to like. I had, after all, dated regularly on most of our posts after I was fourteen. Well, Dad had provided me with his choice and thrown us together by the simple expedient of making the Chosen my guardian, in case he shouldn't be around to introduce us. Of course, Dad was a fatalist so he would have done just as he had to make sure Regan Laird and I met. Had he anticipated the fact that I would divine his complicity? Probably. Dad never underestimated my intelligence, which is why I worked so bloody hard at getting good marks. He'd insisted on a proper good education even to the point of putting me in day schools when the post facilities were inadequate. And he'd insisted I try for Radcliffe. Always aim high, he'd said.

I gave Dad full marks for a mighty shrewd campaign. I wondered if the major had tumbled to Dad's strategy. Probably not. Dad kept his cards hidden. He'd always made money playing poker even against Turtle. But now I understood why the major had been deluded about my sex. Dad had intended to imply that I was a boy so the major would be easily gulled into the guardian routine.

Wait a moment. Did Dad have a precognition of his death? No, I dismissed that notion as foreign to his character. A cautious soldier always leaves a bolt-hole.

Silly tears came to my eyes, tears of longing and gratitude for this silly, magnificent gesture. I turned my head into my pillow and sobbed bitterly for his loss, for the utter wastefulness of his manner of dying. Merlin shifted his body, nuzzling me with ready sympathy. I buried my head in his silky ruff and he endured my rough embrace and sobs with devoted patience. I finally cried myself into an exhausted sleep.

I drifted back to consciousness in a curious state of mind. I had evidently argued with myself while sleeping and I had the silliest impression I was picking up the argument at a point where I had dropped off to sleep. I was saying to myself, as consciousness increased, that if Dad had never underestimated my intelligence, he had overestimated my physical charms. What guarantee had I that I had any appeal for the major? Now there, I found myself commenting, was the crux of the matter. It was all very well for Dad to slap the white man's burden on Major Regan Laird but did he intend to leave the seducing to me? And did my father feel I was up to such carrying-on?

For one thing, I was twenty and the major must be fifteen or so years my senior. If not more. He was a damned good looking man, or would be again, when the surgeons at Walter Reed had a go at him. The good Major Laird might have certain plans in mind that did not include the five feet two inches, one hundred and a half pounds of curly-haired imp. Imp was what I had self-styled myself from the day I had regretfully decided at sixteen that I was stuck down at five feet two inches. The major was a well-built six foot one. The angle of elevation made his height deceptive. It was a pet peeve of mine to see tall men guiding around little girls. It seemed a waste, particularly when I considered some of my lengthy friends forced to wear flats so as not to tower above their dates.

Of course, once this fool war got finished up, taller men might reappear on the scene. In the meantime, it was close to indecent for five foot two to run around under the waistband of six foot one. That was approximately eleven inches going to waste, right there and, as we are forever being told, don't waste manpower. This put me in mind of a very obscene joke I'd overheard. Which put me in a very good frame of mind. Which reminded me of how I had fallen asleep.

My grief over my father had taken a curious shift somewhere during the subconscious moments of the night. Perhaps I had admitted that Dad had forever passed beyond recall. Perhaps I had let go the trappings of grief to take up the banner of just retribution and vengeance. Of perhaps time, in its inevitable way, had moved me past the initial plateau of sorrow. Turtle Bailey's appearance had completed my acceptance, allowing me the vital catharsis of tears coupled with pleasanter reminders.

My remorse over things omitted and committed in relation to Dad had been painfully keen. The letters I had not found time to write that would have reached him in a moment of desolation. The meals I had elected not to spend in his company. All the petty things that rise to plague the mourner were now done with.

It would be ridiculous to chalk up my new spirit to one isolated incident. It seemed plain silly to waste time analyzing the whys and wherefores. Just accept the blessing graciously and get yourself out of bed, I told myself.

I looked at my watch.

"Ten o'clock!" I exclaimed, sitting up. With some astonishment I realized Merlin had left. My exploring hand told me it must have been some time ago for the impression his body had made was cold.

A shutter, its fastening broken or loosened by the continual pounding of the storm winds, swung leisurely ajar. The day was fair with the curious brilliance of reflected snow. Someone had mended the fire again for new logs burned warmly on the grate.

I dragged clean clothes out of my suitcase, loath to leave the warmth of bed. I managed to dress under the bedclothes, no mean feat. I rued the fact that slacks and pullovers are not exactly siren togs but I could not fancy any man enjoying the embrace of an ice maiden, however chic in her dress. Presuming, of course, I could entice the major within my skinny arms in the first place.

I stared at my image in the mirror over the dresser. There had been no overnight physical metamorphosis. I sighed. The color in my cheeks was only the product of the nippy air and the freckles stood out like beauty marks. The dark circles under my green eyes had receded by perhaps a quarter of an inch. I brushed my black hair vigorously, hoping it might condescend to fluff out. Instead, the friction in the cold air only made it lie flatter to my skull. I looked more like Joan of Arc than Helen of Troy. I gave up and decided to put my trust in good cooking, hoping that the major was so suitably indoctrinated into infantryitis as to remember that every army moves on its stomach.

"Forward, Joan," I urged and opened my door with a dramatic flourish.

The major, about to knock, teetered precariously in an effort not to knock on my forehead and to recapture his balance in order not to spill the coffee in his hand.

"And what does Joan have to do with the morning?" he asked, a droll expression in his eyes.

"I have absolutely no idea," I lied. "How sweet of you!" I took the coffee from him gratefully.

He was dressed in an assortment of heavy clothing, widewale corduroy trousers tucked into infantry boots, a well-worn red blanket-coat, sweater cuffs showing at the wrists which indicated he wore several layers under the jacket, a muffler, and a hunting hat with earflaps turned down. Heavy gloves were stuffed in one pocket.

"Don't tell me mine is the only fire in the house?" I . asked, indicating his outdoor costume. He reached over my shoulder, reminding me again of the difference in our heights, and closed the door to my bedroom.

"No. There are several islands against the sub-zero weather," he assured me. "But we won't keep them long if Bailey and I don't bring home some more wood. I neglected to plan on so many houseguests, to say nothing of that storm when I last chopped up a woodpile."

"One of these years we must put in central heating," I said and suppressed the astonishment I felt at hearing myself so possessively impudent.

He hesitated a brief instant, giving me a measuring look before he smiled politely. "Yes, we must." There was the briefest lingering on the pronoun.

With what poise I could muster after that gaffe, I glided to the stairs and hurried to the kitchen, hoping the devil was not at my heels.

Merlin was having words with Turtle when I entered from the hall. Merlin was extremely pleased with himself, his tail pumping violently while he barked fit to clear the chimneys of soot. Turtle, too, was dressed for heavy weather work. He needed the padding to roughhouse with Merlin. The kitchen chairs had been knocked askew and the heavy wood bucket had been pushed back under the kitchen sink.

"Good for you, Turtle," I cheered as Merlin made a lunge which Turtle dodged expertly. "He had to give up that sort of play with me when he was eight months old or there would have been crushed Carlysle to spoon up from the floor. And he loves to fight."

"This dog has 'an insufficiently aggressive temperament'?" asked Regan Laird dryly, hands on his hips, watching the dog's snarling face.

Turtle looked up just long enough to be distracted. Merlin took advantage and sank his teeth into the sergeant's forearm.

"You overgrown son of a bitch," Turtle roared. "Leggo." Merlin promptly obliged.

The sergeant rubbed his forearm thoughtfully, frowning at the dog with new respect. He had felt that bite even through the layers of clothing.

I was laughing too hard to be sympathetic although I did hand signal Merlin to sit. He didn't want to but he did. Glancing at the major, I caught my breath, my laughter trailing off. He had turned up his jacket collar, preparatory to braving the cold outside, and only his good profile showed. I abruptly gave up all hope that I could ever interest him in little old Little Bit.

"Ready, Major?" Turtle picked up an ax from the kitchen table, the edge gleaming with newly sharpened steel. "Keep the coffee hot, Bit," he enjoined me and the two started out.

Merlin whined expectantly, rocking back and forth as he reluctantly maintained the sit. I waved him out.

"Wait a minute. I want him here with you," the major objected, extending his leg across Merlin's path. The shepherd stopped, whining plaintively.

"Oh, for Pete's sweet suffering sake," I exclaimed in exasperation. "And what panzer division are you expecting today?" I waved out the window at the snow-fast land.

The major deliberated, shrugged, and slapped the side of his leg to encourage Merlin. The three stamped out through the back. As they lurched up the slippery slope behind the house into the scrubby beach pines, I saw a sled trailing behind the major. High slatted sides had been fastened on to make it an excellent wood carrier on either snow or sand. Once it must have been young Regan's and I wondered what kind of a boy he'd been.

"Maxim two," I muttered to myself, "the infantry moves on its belly and they will be mighty hungry 'footsojers' when they get back . . . probably on their bellies."

I brought meat in from the freezing porch and eyed it. I might as well pop it into the oven now. Eventually it would have to thaw. I found a pan and, a little dismayed at the size and solidity of the meat, put it in the oven, closed the door, and crossed my fingers.

I remembered seeing some dried apples so I put them to soak and got out pie-crust makings. Oh, but it was nice to have butter to cook with again.

When I put the pie in, there was the barest hint of tan on the meat. Fork testing proved that approximately one thirty-second of an inch had thawed. This was a hopeful sign. I fed the stove a few sticks of wood and did dishes. It then occurred to me that men were men in blizzard and in war. I went to find what I could do with the state of the major's socks, et cetera.

This little job was taken care of and distributed neatly, festooning the bathroom, after a solid hour of scrubbing and rinsing in the tub. The pie had cooked perhaps a trifle too crisply brown but it smelled heavenly. The meat was doing far better than I expected so I fed the stove again and went to straighten up the study.

One of the nicer things about a good fire is that it burns. It burns dust, cigarette butts, and dirt. By the time I had finished, the major's room actually looked respectable. I had also changed the sheets after an intensive recon for a linen closet. I was coming down the stairs with fresh towels when I saw what must have been a snow mirage. I covered my eyes with my hand for a moment and looked out again.

The figure plodding down the road was no mirage. It also walked like an infantryman. I caught the glint of metal at the shoulder, but the face was hunched in the protection of the collar, chin tucked down so that I couldn't distinguish any features.

The more I looked the more apprehensive I became. It was ridiculous to assume the man was looking for any other house but this. All the others were boarded up so tightly and no one would survive in this weather without a fire. Our chimneys were all blooming with smoke.

The stranger was no one I knew. Not even Warren. Not that you'd have caught Warren walking very far. Certainly not in weather like this. Warren loudly bemoaned the fact officers no longer rode thoroughbred steeds into battle, spurring valiantly into the fray, saber held high. He was a frustrated Jeb Stuart-ite. However, he had accepted the jeep as an endurable alternative to walking.

No, this wasn't Warren but it was somebody looking for the major. I deeply regretted my generosity with Merlin. I'd have faced my mythical panzer unit with no qualms with that shepherd at my side.

The man had come abreast of the house now. He looked towards it, examining the sloping approach. He made a decision and started up, removing his hands from his pockets as the tricky footing required additional balance. He slipped and went down on one knee. As he got to his feet I saw his face for the first time. He was no one I knew but his face, not handsome like the major's, was attractive and there was an openness in the exasperated determination on his face that I liked.

I threw back the bolts on the front door and pulled it open.

"May I help you?" I asked, conscious of the triteness of that remark.

He looked up, startled, grinned broadly as he brushed snow off his legs.

"You sure can, Mrs. Laird," he agreed warmly with a trace of a southern accent in his tone. "You are Mrs. Laird, aren't you?" he asked with concern when he saw the startled expression on my face.

"No!" I said flatly, wondering if I looked that old in the light.

"I beg your pardon, ma'am, but this is Major Regan Laird's house. Or did I take the wrong turn?" and he looked over his shoulder at the road in dismay.

"No, this is the right house."

He was almost to the front door now, and the ground under the drifts was even. He got up to the windswept front stoop and stamped the snow off his boots and trousers.

"Actually, while I do want to see the major, I was told that his ward, James Murdock, would be here."

"That's right."

"I served with the lad's father in France," he said quietly, "and I wanted to see him."

"That does you credit," I said, gesturing at the drifts and trying not to sound sarcastic.

He regarded me with a disconcerting directness in his clear light-green eyes.

"May I come in? I'd hate to cool the house off," and, at my invitation, he pushed the door wider and stepped in.

"There's not an appreciable difference in this part of the house," I explained, suddenly aware of the load of towels in my arms. "Follow me, Lieutenant . . . ?"

"DeLord, Robert DeLord, ma'am."

The towels fell in a mosaic on the floor as I turned to stare at him, the temperature within me matching that of this part of the house.

8

"I'M SORRY. Did I do that?" he apologized, bending quickly to pick up the towels before the snow from his boots could melt into them. I held out my arm stupidly while he piled them up.

"The kitchen is warm," I managed to say and, in a daze, led the way.

"Apple pie," he exclaimed, sniffing deeply as he entered. "That smells good and proper."

"Been back long?" I asked inanely, putting the towels down on the cabinet and getting a mug down for him. My inner thoughts were too chaotic to sort out. I had the feeling of being on a treadmill. I had to keep moving faster or I'd fall off altogether. Like Alice, running as fast as she could to stay in the same place. Only, as of right now, I wasn't even in the same place.

"Got in a week ago," he replied genially.

"Take your things off."

He divested himself, grinning apologetically as he kept peeling off layers. When he had got down to uniform tunic, he turned to take the coffee I poured him.

"Just black, thank you, ma'am," he smiled and edged close to the stove. "That was one mighty cold walk," he continued sociably, his glance dropping to the pie and away. "I got a lift from the railroad station to the first crossroads. The Coast Guard. Oh, near forgot, the station master gave me some mail for the major and young Murdock," he said, and having found the letters in his pocket, handed them over to me. "Special Delivery." His grin was frank and broad.

"You weren't kidding." A stupid remark, for one of them, addressed to me, was liberally covered with special delivery stamps. It was from Mrs. Everett and thick. She had probably forwarded me some letters, I thought. It was sweet of her to go to so much trouble. I put the letters down on the sideboard.

"No, ma'am," he said, turning this way and that to warm all angles of him at the stove.

He had crisp blond hair cut close to his scalp, and I could see the line of a bullet crease along the top of his head. He was stockily built and shorter than the major but still six or seven inches the better of me. He seemed to he waiting expectantly and I realized he wondered why I didn't call "the Murdock lad" or the major.

"The men are out after wood," I explained hastily and gestured him to the chair nearest the stove. He thanked me again and sat down, hands curled around the hot mug.

"You sure would need it, day like today."

"Day like the last several."

"Ah," he began self-consciously, clearing his throat, "how's the kid taking his father's . . . death?"

"I think I'd better set you straight, Lieutenant DeLord," I said deliberately. He looked apprehensive. I held up my hand. "Now this may come as a surprise to you but—I'm James Carlysle Murdock."

"Well, I'm pleased to . . ." and he did a perfect double take. "Did I hear you right, ma'am? You're James Carlysle Murdock?"

"Oh, yes, if you knew my father for very long, lieutenant or very well, you probably discovered he had an odd sense of humor."

The light green eyes regarded me seriously.

"He was also somewhat stubborn. He had chosen an appropriate name for his firstborn, so it didn't occur to him to change the name simply because he was disappointed in the sex of the child. I have been James Carlysle Murdock all my life and there have been limes, especially since Pearl Harbor, when it has been a liability, believe me."

The green eyes began to twinkle although the face had not changed expression. The twinkle turned to laughter and then the mouth turned up at the corners as Lieutenant DeLord started to laugh. He continued to laugh until the infectious quality of his mirth caught me up, too, dispersing entirely my apprehension about him.

"James Carlysle Murdock, well, that's one on me," he said.

"No," I contradicted him, grinning, "that's one on me."

This set him off again and I joined in so wholeheartedly that neither of us heard the men approaching until the back door burst open and Merlin came charging into the room.

The moment the shepherd saw the newcomer he changed from a happy dog in from a mad morning of fun into a guard animal, alert, intent, moving slowly, purposefully, towards the stranger.

I'll say this for DeLord, he didn't move a muscle. It took a strong will not to retreat from the sight he was facing.

"At ease, Merlin!" I said sharply.

The hackles on Merlin's back dropped, his muscles relaxed and he came forward at a normal pace, to sniff the hand DeLord slowly extended.

"Friend," I added, having just decided that. Merlin was already making a new acquaintance.

This had all happened very quickly so that both Turtle and the major had just reached the doorway when Merlin touched DeLord's hand with an inquisitive nose. DeLord got to his feet.

"The lieutenant, by God," Turtle ground out.

"Major," the lieutenant acknowledged gravely. "Bailey. Didn't realize you were back, sergeant."

"No, sir, just got back. Excuse me, Major," and Turtle pushed in with the load of logs he was lugging.

Regan Laird, also laden, came in too, hooking the door shut with his foot. There was a clatter as Turtle dropped his burden into the wood basket.

What brings you to this neck of the woods?" the major asked, stalking—yes, that was the term—stalking across to dump his own load.

"Young James Carlysle Murdock," drawled the lieutenant, moving to one side to let the men warm themselves at the stove. He leaned back, against the inner wall, one hand holding the coffee mug, the other thrust into his pocket. He seemed far more at ease than either the major or Turtle.

At the mention of my full name, the major frowned, first at me and then at the lieutenant.

"He thought I was Mrs. Laird," I giggled nervously.

"Issat apple pie?" Turtle cried, pointing to it.

"No," I told him, making a face, "it's monkey meat."

Turtle grinned, turning to Laird with a satisfied smile.

"I tol'ya we'd eat good when we got back."

I pushed them both out of the way to check on the roast. The fork went in smoothly, two full inches.

"I'd have given odds this meat wouldn't thaw before late tomorrow," I commented, closing the door slowly on the delicious aroma. I was very conscious of the major's alertness, DeLord's almost insolent ease, and the fact that Turtle wanted to improve the situation.

"Yorkshire pudding?" Turtle asked hopefully.

"If this ever cooks," I promised, poking the meat again. "It'll probably be red-raw in the middle."

"Only way to eat it," Turtle replied, rubbing his hands together and licking his lips. "Right, Major?"

"Yes," the major agreed absently. "Could we have some coffee, Carlysle?"

"Yes, yes." I went to the cupboard, planting my hands on the counter to lever myself up.

"The stool, Carlysle. Use the stool," the major said in a grating voice that sounded more like Turtle's.

"Allow me," said the lieutenant smoothly and handed me down two mugs. I thanked him sweetly, carefully avoiding Regan Laird's eyes. The air fairly crackled with his annoyance.

"The lieutenant hitched a ride in with the Coast Guard," I said conversationally as I filled the mugs. "He brought us some mail, too. Special delivery." I glanced over at DeLord with a special grin for our inside joke.

Picking up the packet of letters, I rifled through them. Two for Regan Laird were in the brown manila envelopes, franked for official business, U.S. Army. There were two Vmail envelopes for me plus Mrs. Everett's letter and one with a local postmark.

"If you'll excuse me a minute, I'll see what my nice landlady has to say," I said, drawing up a chair to the far end of the table, "since she was 'specialing' it to me."

One envelope, addressed in an unfamiliar handwriting, fell out of the pages and pages of lined tablet paper that had been folded over it.

"Jesus," I exclaimed angrily, "what does that bastard want with me?"

"Bit, can it," Turtle growled at me.

I pursed my lips. "Warren!" I flung the envelope distastefully to the table, "Guardian, *you* read it."

I picked up Mrs. Everett's bulky pages; her platitudes and homey admonitions ought to calm me down. I had got the first four phrases deciphered when I realized what she was babbling about.

"Good heavens," I cried out, staring at the men. "Someone did get in the house. Mrs. Everett says my room was torn apart. Damn," I added because she went on to say that all my college notes had been thrown around the room.

> *All your books* [I read on] *were scattered and it was the most awful mess. Really, Carla, I was terribly upset. Naturally Father insisted on calling the police and they came and questioned every one of us. I felt simply awful. I don't know what the neighbors will think, much less your dean. They are so particular at the college where the girls stay. And it was only your room that was searched. That's what the police say. That your room was searched. I know you'll be hearing from them because they have to know what might be missing. I explained to the detective that you were convalescing on Cape Cod with your guardian. I told him that you had left only your books because you were not to study, but rest. But I didn't want you to think that we aren't careful of your things. You know how I always lock*

*the doors, particularly since we had that scare be-
fore. You know, dear Carla, I find I miss that dog
when things like this can happen. He may have upset me a little when you first came here, but I can
see now why he's been such a comfort to you.*

Upset was a euphemism for scared sick. Her fear of the dog
had warred with her desire to mother the war orphan. I had
sensed this and had waved the flag violently. Considering how
most army personnel were treated before the war, I had no com-
punctions about exploiting the new status.

Mrs. Everett did not believe in paragraphs nor in much
punctuation. Her style, while very like her, lacked the addition
al flavor of her broad Dorchester accent, but I had a vivid picture of her standing indignantly before me as I read the letter.
Embarrassed over the notoriety, concerned over the possible re-
percussions on her carefully maintained reputation

*So don't be alarmed, Carla, when the police call
to ask you about your things. Kay Alexander was so
sweet and came and helped me pick things up and
put the room back together again. You'll be glad to
know that nothing was really damages* [I interpreted this to mean the furnishings and linens escaped harm] *and everything is back in place just as
you like it.*

*Now, I know Mrs. Laird will cook good nourish-
ing meal for you. I always said you never ate
enough to keep a bird alive and you so [she had
crossed out a word with many lines] slim anyway.*

I looked up from my letter, having deleted the last para
graph from my running commentary of her remarks. The major
was scowling, Turtle growled deep in his throat, sounding like
Merlin, and the lieutenant was watching. Just watching, but
was certain no detail on anyone's reaction missed his scrutiny.

"Was there anything you wouldn't like to find missing?' asked Regan Laird slowly.

"I told you," I began, "I brought everything down here but books, as ordered," and I glared at him, "and you have the. . . ." The look on the major's face stopped me. "That's the trouble with majors," I complained to the lieutenant, trying to make this sudden switch appear spontaneous. If the major was worried about DeLord's possible complicity with Warren, I had already said too much. But the expression on DeLord's face was one of polite interest, nothing more. "The trouble with majors," I repeated, giving Laird a dirty look, "is that they don't have enough responsibility to make them humble and too much authority to make them human."

DeLord burst out laughing. This certainly wouldn't improve his relations with Laird but when Turtle joined in, the major had to grin at my deprecating description.

"You have to get up early to put one over on Little Bit," Turtle announced proudly. "But I don't like this burglary."

I shrugged. "There wasn't anything for him to take but, if my Government 18 notes are all fouled up, I'll. . . ." I trailed off as I saw the major opening Warren's letter.

He read it quickly, the muscles around his mouth tightening with distaste. He tossed it over to me.

"Innocuous enough," he said in a flat voice.

I thought I caught a gleam of interest in DeLord's eyes but he maintained his incurious pose.

I didn't pick the letter up. For one thing it had floated to my side of the table, right side up, so I wasn't forced to touch it to read it.

I made an impolite sound in my throat as I read the opening paragraph:

> *Dear Carla,*
>
> *Marian and I wish to express again our deeply sympathy for your orphaned state. I admired your father . . .*

"You hated his guts!"

. . . and respected his ability to command . . .

"Which is why you often ignored his orders and snafued everything with your own."

I was deeply shocked and grieved at his death.

"You probably got roaring drunk with delight."

You may not have heard that I sustained a wound in Aachen.

"And hoped you were! With no pain-killers."

. . . and have been relieved, temporarily you may be sure, of my command.

"Permanently unless Bradley wants the V Corps to go mass AWOL."

Marian and I happen to be coming to Boston on the 28th . . .

"I wonder which general's wife she's sucking up to now." "Carlysle!" The major snapped .

. . . and would very much like to see you for old time's sake. I will call when we arrive and arrange a date.

> *Affectionately yours,*
> *LT COL. DONALD H. WARREN*

"Affectionately? He debased the word."

DeLord's green eyes were sparking and the hint of a grin twitched at his lips.

"Well," I said with great satisfaction, "isn't it a pity I missed them? My timing is superb." I flicked a finger at the letter and it drifted across the table to Turtle. "Burn it, Bailey."

Turtle was about to comply when the major retrieved it. He replaced it in the envelope.

"You know Colonel Warren?" DeLord asked me with the most innocent expression I have ever seen on a lieutenant's face. Even Turtle blinked respectfully.

"Carlysle," the major cautioned me, his eyes angry.

"I'm all too well acquainted with Lieutenant Colonel Warren," I replied, stressing the rank with acid scorn, ignoring my guardian deliberately. "The very idea that he was given my father's command—even far a day—turns my stomach."

"Carlysle!" the major said more forcefully.

DeLord's expectant look was an added goad to my defiance.

"I was ignored by him until I reached adolescence and learned, like every other young girl on the post, to keep something solid between me and him. I've been condescendingly chaperoned and mothered," I shuddered violently, "by his dear Marian, who'd sell herself to a corporal if it would look good on her Donnie's 201 file."

This time the major grabbed me by the arm and shook me. I swung around long enough to wrench my arm free.

"I'm not army anymore and I can say what I want to now about Lieutenant Colonel Donald Warren. And I can say it to whomever I please!"

Merlin began to growl in his throat.

"You see, the dog agrees. He'd love to sink his teeth into Warren and I wouldn't call him off. Warren's had it coming a long, long time."

"That is quite enough from you, young lady," the major said in a steely voice. He meant it and for one fleeting second I was positive he'd slap me across the mouth if I said one more word.

Considering he had a very poor opinion of Warren, I couldn't see why he objected until I recalled that he, or Turtle, had mentioned that DeLord had been thick with Warren after Dad's death. Well, green-eyed DeLord would bloody well know where I stood as far as Warren was concerned. Discretion be damned.

Turtle had kept his mouth shut during my tirade. DeLord had ducked his head as if that would help him avoid participating in the tense scene. I saw DeLord tenderly finger the bullet score on his head as if it suddenly bothered him.

"Well," I said, turning my attack to him, "now how do you think James Carlysle Murdock is adjusting to her father's death?"

The lieutenant shot me a penetrating look, compounded of surprise and shock. I saw him dart a glance at Laird and then at Turtle. He pulled himself back into the pose he adopted—I was sure now it was a pose—and laughed nervously.

"No comment."

"Chicken!"

He threw up both hands in a mock defense. "I'll take krauts any day against a colonel's daughter." For the first time I noticed the West Point ring on his finger.

"A typical career man's remark!" I scoffed. "It just volunteered you for KP, Turtle, we need wood everywhere."

"Sounds like the colonel, too," DeLord muttered good naturedly to Turtle. "Yes, sir, ma'am, sir," he said, saluting me repeatedly.

"I'll unload the sled," the major offered before I could pointedly ignore him in my summary disposition of duties.

"Dinner in an hour, with Yorkshire pudding," and I cocked a finger at Turtle.

One of the basic facts I had learned from the years with my father was that occasionally men enjoy being ordered around by a woman. Just occasionally. Whether it's a voluntary return to the status of small, naughty boys or whether it's just a relief not to have to make decisions, I don't know. But I often found it worked with my father. However, he was quick enough to tell me when I was out of line, if I did not sense it first.

I seized upon this ploy because I wanted some time to think. I wanted the air to clear between Major Laird and myself, now that the unexpected arrival of DeLord had erased the nice sense of companionship between Turtle, Laird, and me.

Whatever those two said, I could not place Robert DeLord in Warren's camp. He was a very cool man and his green eyes missed nothing. I was certain he was sensitive to a lot of what was not being discussed.

The major did not seem to trust him nor want him to know that we suspected Dad had been murdered—there, I could actually think it without wincing—and that all my father's effects were under this roof. It was compatible with the respect in which my father's men had held him that they would make the duty call, however painful, on his daughter were they able to. That sufficiently explained DeLord's reason for seeking me out. I had myself, at Dad's instigation, made several calls on Boston families of combat fatalities. I had been rather surprised to learn that Mrs. Colonel Warren had also paid such visits. She didn't live in Boston. I wondered what had got into her. Bucking for Warren's chicken wings, probably.

In the meantime, I set the lieutenant to peeling potatoes.

"I didn't really intend to impose on your hospitality, Miss Carlysle."

"Carla," I corrected automatically. I couldn't get that message through to the major but the lieutenant was going to start out right.

"Carla."

"And don't give me any nonsense about imposing. If a man has the decency to hunt up his colonel's daughter, he is entitled to one good meal. Especially when he braves blizzards to pay his respects."

"Yes, ma'am," was all he said to that but his eyes sparkled.

I didn't want him to get the idea that I was too stupid to realize he had some double purpose.

"How long is your leave?" I went on, not letting him reform his thoughts.

"Oh, I'm entitled to quite a bit," he temporized.

"You're peeling them too thick. Didn't you learn anything at the Point?"

His grin widened. He concentrated on his peeling.

"I certainly look forward to a piece of your apple pie." He reverted to his original trend of thought.

"Yes, I'd noticed."

He stopped peeling a moment, looking at the middle distance as he reflected.

"It's funny ma'am, apple pie was one of the things you're supposed to miss."

I snorted.

"Actually, what I craved most was an Idaho baked potato!"

"Not hominy grits?"

He gave me a rueful grin. "I keep trying to live down my rebel origins. No, a baked potato, hot and fluffy inside, with buckets of butter!"

"The major must have an 'in' with the local cow," I commented, showing him the wheel of butter.

His eyes widened with delight at such a supply.

"In Europe," he continued, peeling carefully, "the potatoes are small and yellow. When you can get 'em at all. Oh, all right in stews and such but they don't bake." He turned the potato over in his hand. The russet was not exactly in prime condition nor very large, but the flesh was white. "Your father was a good rough cook. Did you know?"

I snorted. "And who do you think taught him?"

"I got a few days off in October and made for Paree." I expected him to respond to his reminiscences in some typically military fashion, a smirk, a smile, or a grimace. But he went on, "And, of all people, guess who I met?" He slapped his thigh for emphasis, a gesture entirely out of character. "Who did I run into but Colonel Murdock? Never guessed then he'd be my C.O. in a few weeks' time. And guess where?"

"You tell me."

He looked at me squarely for a moment, wonderingly.

"Buying stamps!"

He paused and deliberately finished peeling the potato. I said nothing.

"Yes, ma'am. We were fellow philatelists." He glanced up at me. "He was lucky that day. He picked up some departing German officer's abandoned collection. Has it been returned to you?"

He was regarding me squarely, his eyes on mine, his face grave.

"Yes, Lieutenant, it has." I failed to add that the two onion-skin lists were in my pocket, one with his name in pencil at the top.

He heaved a counterfeit sigh of relief. It irritated me beyond measure that he continued his playacting. He must be aware I was not fooled by it.

"I'm very glad, Miss Carla, because I know some of those stamps were valuable. Your father was very pleased to get the French-Chinese 1900 issues."

That gave me pause for those were some of the items Dad had listed and checked off.

"I was afraid," the lieutenant continued, concentrating on his potato for a moment, "that it might have gone astray in the shuffle at Division HQ. Or that someone might have offered you a good price for it?" He gave me a quick look.

"The peels are getting thick again." I remarked caustically.

He paid attention to his peeling.

"Or maybe," he suggested softly, "you know enough about stamps to realize the collection is valuable?"

"Yes, I do know Dad's stamps are valuable."

"The ones he got in France?" and DeLord scanned my face.

"I haven't gone through them closely but I thank you for the warning. No one will get them without paying a lot for them."

We were looking directly in each other's eyes now. I couldn't tell what he was thinking or what reaction he had been trying to get from me. He was forewarned, at any rate, if his part in all this was devious.

I had a sudden urge to level with Robert DeLord completely. I disliked underhanded dealings and hidden meanings. I liked things open and understood. I preferred to know where I stood with people and I wanted them to know where they were with me. My instinct was to trust DeLord. Dad had. He might even have trusted DeLord with information he didn't pass on to Turtle or the major for some peculiar reason. He might even have charged DeLord with keeping an eye on Warren—which would account for DeLord's interest in that man. If Dad had been conscious as DeLord had been bringing him back in the jeep, he might have told DeLord something, even who murdered him. And if DeLord had buddy-buddied Warren . . . maybe there was a damned good reason. It would certainly explain DeLord's line of questioning as well as his efforts to reach me. And the major? Oh, no. No!

"Good," DeLord was saying, accepting my implied warning.

"By any chance," I replied, twisting my dig a little, "would you be interested in buying them?"

"Me? No, ma'am," he answered with honest surprise. "Not on a lieutenant's pay."

Turtle came in. He looked sardonically at the lieutenant's labor but said nothing, passing through to the back porch. I heard him rumbling on to the major. The conversation with DeLord had been punctuated with the cracks of an ax against wood and the thud as logs were piled against the side of the back porch. As I heard the clumping of several pairs of feet approaching, I switched to more general conversation. I could see that it rubbed my guardian exactly the wrong way to find me and Robert DeLord in congenial good spirits. I paid Major Regan Laird no attention whatsoever as he stood peeling off layers of clothing.

"Sun's over the yardarm, Turtle," I announced when the sergeant came in.

I ignored Turtle's startled look at the use of his nickname. He shot a menacing glance at the lieutenant who did not so much as flutter a muscle. The sobriquet might never be used by anyone but me but I'll bet anything the whole regiment knew it.

"Gotta wash," the sergeant mumbled. He and the major disappeared.

I listened for the major's explosion when he entered the bathroom. His profanity, muffled but unmistakable, startled the lieutenant. I gave him no explanation and continued blithely to set the table as I pumped him.

"You never saw Camp . . . Fort Dix . . . I'll never get that straight," I groaned, "before its new exalted position, did you?"

"No, Miss Carla."

"Just Holabird and Benning?"

"That's right."

"But Holabird was provost marshall school, wasn't it?"

"Oh, I reckon so, but they took in other units just before Pearl, about the time I got there."

"I see." And I was beginning to. And I wondered if I liked that conclusion. If Major Laird and Turtle had their doubts about DeLord, maybe they had a good reason, apart from the one they gave, for distrusting him. But Dad hadn't and, as regimental C.O., he would have known that DeLord was provost marshal. But why should a secret PM be attached to the regiment? Warren had pulled an awfully costly blunder at Bois de Collette in the Cotentin Peninsula that had decimated two companies, but to warrant a PM? No. There had been some extenuating circumstances. If Dad had only got rid of Warren . . . the man had been an albatross forever. He had a way of giving orders that positively antagonized officer and enlisted man alike. He was the greatest refugee from the Civil War since Custer and he never had been able to understand the necessity for changing tactics that had been successful in Napoleon's day. For instance, the need for tank support of infantry (Warren, Dad had told me, considered tanks a Buck Roger's lunacy) and the necessity of sustaining an artillery barrage until visible casualties among your own men—these new tricks of warfare Warren simply could not accept. But Dad had gone to the Point with Warren and Dad had his own Scotch ideas of loyalty. Well, they had cost him his life. Did DeLord suspect that? That would have brought down a provost marshal. But DeLord had been with the regiment long before that. Why?

Nor could I see any connection between provost marshal and a perfectly respectable stamp hobby. Not unless Dad had taken blocks of stamps from the French postal service and they were raising a Gallic fuss. But Dad was discriminating and large blocks didn't interest him. And, anyway, Dad had been in Paris before DeLord joined the outfit, not after. So it wasn't stamps . . . exactly. . . .

I heard the major's heavy step in the corridor. There was no mistaking the suppressed anger in that determined thump. I wondered if he wanted to rake me over the coals for doing the laundry, or for festooning it in the bathroom. At any rate, he was livid, or the scar was a very reliable pressure gauge. And I just didn't care.

It did seem a little ungrateful of him when you considered the efforts I had saved his majorial dignity. I couldn't picture him bending over a steamy washboard. And there is nothing like combat boots to foul up socks for fair. But oh, he was mad.

Fortunately, DeLord's presence was inhibiting and, though the major's eyes blazed with fury, he said nothing. He stalked over to the cabinet and got out three glasses. I was about to remind him there were four of us when he swung his body around, shot a frown at DeLord, and took down one more.

"Soda?" he barked at the lieutenant.

"Neat!"

This, too, annoyed the major. He put the glasses on the table with a thud which roused Merlin. He had been snoozing under the table but sat upright with a throaty growl, aware of the undercurrent in the room.

Major Laird, until that moment unaware of Merlin's presence, sprang backwards, hunching, his hand automatically seeking a nonexistent gunbutt at his hip, all his combat reflexes alerted by the unexpected noise. For one split second I wondered if he would be foolhardy enough to lash out at Merlin. Even as that outrageous thought cross my mind, I realized how unworthy it was. Mad at me the major might be, but he was not the sort of person who slapped down the next guy in line for someone else's fault.

"Easy, fella," he said although the admonition went to the wrong person. Merlin sneezed and lay back down.

I wondered if the major realized he looked a trifle foolish, at least to me he did, overreacting to a dog's growl. I glanced at the lieutenant out of the corner of my eye. I amended my thought and decided I was foolish. The lieutenant approved the major's quickness. It was analogous to Turtle's reflex attack on me yesterday. I was the one at fault, I chided myself, being very childish, selfish and thoughtless. These men had been in combat. Their nerves were still wire-tight and battle-honed. I had no right to play on their emotions and set up situations that increased their tensions.

"Oh," I exclaimed, as if suddenly remembering, "I'm sorry about the bathroom, Major. I left stuff all over. I hope you didn't mind my taking over like that. Force of habit. I always did it for Dad."

"Thank you," the major said stiffly, his head barely inclining in my direction. "It was kindly meant, I'm sure, but unnecessary."

"Dry yet?"

He shook his head and continued fixing the drinks. Turtle barged into the kitchen.

"Freezing upstairs," he croaked, warming his hands over the stove.

The major handed drinks around. The lieutenant hopped up nimbly for a man who affected a languorous attitude most of the time.

"The colonel, God bless him," grated out Turtle, raising his glass. It still had the quality of a prayer, not a toast. Was Turtle getting religion?

My inner question helped me over the moment. No tears and only a slight constriction in my throat, so it surprised me to see a grimness in the lieutenant's mouth. It passed so quickly I may have been reading more than was there.

Turtle reversed a chair as he usually did, and, seeing Merlin sprawled under the table, arranged his feet carefully.

"Wore him out, we did," the sergeant laughed, taking a long swig. "Good stuff. By God, good stuff."

"I didn't realize that shepherds had retriever instincts," was the major's comment, relaxing for the first time since the lieutenant's arrival.

"Oh, Merlin is full of surprises. Did you think to make a sled dog out of him on the way back? He's strong enough to pull quite a heavy load."

Turtle cleared his throat, grinning wickedly at the major.

"We tried," the sergeant admitted.

The major grinned, glancing under the table.

"He didn't seem to think too much of the idea."

"He's been cooped up so much lately, he may just have needed the run," I decided.

"Swim," the major corrected me. "He didn't stay in long, though."

I laughed heartily. "He's a frustrated lifeguard. I remember one time Dad and I went over to Wildwood Beach . . . that's Jersey coast. Merlin wouldn't let me in the water. The sea wasn't rough or anything and Merlin'd been in. We couldn't understand it. Then Dad tried and he wouldn't let Dad in. Dad was furious. A boy, about four or five, started to wade in and Merlin ran around him until the child was so terrified he went screaming back to his parents. I want to tell you we had quite a time. The lifeguards called the police and wouldn't listen when Dad and I kept trying to explain that Merlin was not rabid, had had all his shots, was a trustworthy animal and . . . you know." I nodded significantly at Turtle who nodded back sagely. "They were all set to take Merlin by force when someone started screaming out in the ocean. Come to find out, Merlin wasn't so stupid. There were swarms of jellyfish and men-of-war coming in with the tide." I shuddered at the thought of those slimy, stinging tentacles. "How Merlin knew they constituted a danger, I don't know. But he wasn't going to let me or Dad or that child in the water. The others, already swimming, I guess he figured he couldn't help."

"Dog's near human," the lieutenant commented appreciatively.

Merlin, who knew we were talking about him, laughed happily up at us, his tongue dangling sideways out of his mouth.

The eggy aroma of Yorkshire pudding now overlaid the combined smells of meat and wood smoke. I hastily checked my dinner.

"Sure do admire pioneer women, coping with these things," I groaned, trying to avoid the blast of hot air from the oven. ° We got to eat right now."

"No complaints here," Turtle assured me.

9

MERLIN WOKE ME. The very manner in which he woke me, his cold nose butting into my eyes, told me he was on the alert. He kept butting me in the neck when he saw my eyes open. Assured I was awake, he carefully got down from the bed, turned back, and imperiously nudged my shoulder. Shivering, I dragged my dressing robe around my shoulders and slid into it. Merlin went to the door. No sound, not so much as the click of a toenail on the bare floor.

I opened the door cautiously, grimacing at the effort of keeping the metal latch silent. He slipped out as soon as there was enough space for his body. He went towards the back of the house. I grabbed his neckchain as we passed Turtle's door. I hesitated briefly. Merlin's manner told me someone unannounced was either in the house or trying to get in. He had not barked but had awakened me for further orders. I couldn't imagine who was trying to get in the house, snowbound and isolated as it was.

Even if Lieutenant DeLord, presumably fast asleep in the kitchen as the other two bedrooms had no fireplaces, were prowling about, Merlin was not likely to have been alarmed. He trusted DeLord and had been given no orders restricting the lieutenant to the kitchen.

I'm sure if the major had known I could specify DeLord was to be kept kitchenbound by Merlin, he would have suggested it. But we had had a very convivial evening after all. I don't know when the men got to bed, because I left early. They were well into the bottle when I went up. Perhaps, in their cups, Major Laird might have reconciled his differences with Robert DeLord.

Also, if Lieutenant DeLord was so fascinated by my father's stamps, there were easier ways for him to get a look at them than crawling around a frigid house in the dark. The albums could be anywhere.

So here I was, prowling the freezing hall myself. I paused by Turtle's door and listened, ear against the cold wood. I was rewarded with the sound of fantastic snores, each bigger or more intricately breathed than the last. I was not going to wake him if the only way I could do was to yell "Sarge" or risk my brains blown out.

I passed the room by. Merlin stopped at the bathroom. I could see his eyes gleam as he turned his head back to me expectantly. I tried to remember if the roof of the kitchen extended below the bathroom. Someone could climb it to the second story. If someone had scouted the first floor, he would have seen the lieutenant asleep in the kitchen and decided against that. The back door wasn't locked though the front was, an unnecessary precaution in this weather and on the Cape. No, the back room, where the footlockers were, gave onto the kitchen roof, not this bathroom.

I snapped my finger softly at Merlin and started towards the back room, certain now that would be the point of entry. The next thing I knew someone's hand was over my mouth and I was being yanked back into the bathroom.

I struggled, wondering with amazement why Merlin wasn't ferociously attacking my assailant. I tried to bite the hand over my mouth just as I heard him snap "Quiet!" in a tonelessness that was too low on the audible threshold to be called a whisper. It was the major. He was fully dressed except for boots and wore his heavy outer coat. He had a gun in his hand, a little Luger from the size of it. His lips were at my ear and he released my mouth.

"What's wrong?" he asked in a below-sound word that was really enunciated air.

"Merlin's on the alert," I said, trying to duplicate his near-silent communication. "Why are you here?" I demanded.

"Not now." And, steely fingers around my arm, he propelled me to the back room, Merlin padding soundlessly beside us.

The door creaked as the cold hinges complained in the wood. Then Merlin erupted into the room, launching himself, a silvery projectile, against the back window. There was no doubting the presence of the intruder. His body was silhouetted in the window against the snow on the slope behind the house. Merlin had leaped in silence but the moment he connected with the barrier of glass he burst into enraged snarls. The figure hesitated only briefly and then turned slipping down the incline of the roof and dropping off into the drifted snow below. Merlin clawed frantically at the window, snarling, bilked of an immediate capture. He had more wit than we did, for he did an end-for-end switch to get out of the room and down the stairs.

But the room was small and crowded, with one hundred twenty pounds of shepherd, me in a full-skirted robe, and the major. The door got closed. The major and I in a comedy of errors both tried to find the latch and let the frantic dog out. When we did, Merlin tore around the hallway, no attempt at quiet progress now. He didn't stop at the front door and even as the major, a few steps ahead of me all the time, followed him, we heard Merlin crashing against the kitchen door, barking urgently.

Just as the major reached the kitchen door it opened, revealing the lieutenant, hair tousled, down to his heavy underwear, obviously not the one who had tried to enter the back room. He stepped aside for Merlin and the major. Merlin, his feet scrabbling an impatient tattoo, danced at the back door. The major, his arm fully extended, flipped up the latch and followed the dog's mad flight to the final door out. Merlin took off across the snow with my voice roaring a command after him.

"Hold him, Merlin, hold him and guard!"

As the major started after the dog, I screamed at him, "Your boots. Get your boots. Merlin'll hold whoever it is."

The major caught at the door frame to stop his forward momentum as he, too, realized he was no good in that deep snow in stocking feet. Before he could, I had rushed into the study and retrieved his boots by the fireplace. He dropped to the floor, jamming his feet in, lacing them part way.

The lieutenant was no laggard. He had thrown on pants,

shirt, boots, and jacket. He was out after the major before Turtle, roused by the barking and clatter, entered the kitchen, also dressing as he ran. He was somewhat hampered by the service revolver in one hand.

The three men, almost evenly spaced in their order of pursuit, staggered and plunged through the drifts, guided by Merlin's clear cry.

Shivering as much from cold as excitement, I stood in the doorway, straining to follow the chase. But the night was moonless and the snow cast up deceiving images. I waited, frustrated, angry, hopeful.

I heard Merlin's now distant bark change to an attacking snarl. Despite the confusion in the room and all the doors, he had made up the burglar's head start.

A shot rang out in the still night. I gasped, leaned against the door for support. I heard another shot. Then two more in quick succession, I heard a motor revving and the squeal of protesting metal. Another shot and then a pained yip.

I sank, stricken, to the cold planking of the porch, grabbing the doorframe until I felt my fingernails bend at the quick from the pressure. Merlin! Not Merlin, too! Oh, please God, let me hear him bark, or snarl, or even yip again.

More shots broke the night stillness. I closed my eyes, limp with despair.

"Kill him, kill him," I heard myself shriek. "If he's hurt Merlin, kill him. *Kill him!*"

And then I curled in on myself, sobbing. I couldn't have sat there very long but I might have. The convulsions of wild crying gave way to the violent shaking of shivers. The tears were runnels of ice down my face. I got myself to my feet and forced myself to stop crying. I closed the porch door. I went back to the door of the major's room and closed it. I marched woodenly into the kitchen, closed the door behind me. I leaned against it for a moment, shaking with cold. Then I closed the hall door Turtle had left open. I drew the curtains. I went over to the table and lit the kerosene light, its bright glow a false note in the room. I threw wood on the fire. I couldn't stop shivering so I took the whiskey bottle and poured myself a stiff shot. I stood there, trying to swallow the first mouthful, dreading what the men would tell me when they returned.

Over and over in my brain spun prayer words for Merlin. It wasn't fair, it just wasn't fair, for Merlin to be taken from me, too. Memories of him as a long-eared awkward pup crowded into mind. The foolishness, the folly, the fun of the insolent intelligent beastie. The trials I had undergone to keep him by me from crowded baggage cars to the sometimes third-rate boardinghouses that would accept pets. The times when Dad's allotment check didn't reach me and we had little to eat, too proud to approach acquaintances. All the many, many facets of a relationship that was blessed with an uncanny rapport, transcending his lack of speech. I could not be deprived of that by so mean an instrument as a petty burglar.

I heard motion outside the kitchen. Disregarding the blackout, I spread myself flat against the window, straining to see but the light within the room made the outside indistinct. All I saw were two figures carrying something. I whirled to snatch the porch door open.

"He's hurt but not badly," the major said swiftly, as he and DeLord edged sideways to bring the limp dog-body in.

I swept the lamp from the table, holding it high so they could put Merlin down. I clamped my teeth on my lips, covered my mouth to dampen the sound of the sobs rising in my throat. I widened my eyes to keep them clear of tears.

"Hold the light over here, Miss Carla," the lieutenant ordered, pointing to Merlin's head. He was bending over the dog, shedding his gloves and jacket so he could work better. "He got creased in the scalp. Like me," and he threw me a hasty reassuring grin, "and, I think, in the shoulder. Major, got a first-aid kit?"

"Coming."

The lieutenant's hands were quick but gentle as he felt the unconscious dog's shoulder.

"Yeah, here. Oohoo, that's quite a furrow. Hold the light a little higher."

The major returned, another lamp in one hand, first-aid kit in the other. In the augmented light, the gash was visible, and more.

"He's got a slug in him," the lieutenant said, his fingers locating the lump. "Not deep, though," he reassured me.

When the major put an arm around me, I realized I was swaying. I caught myself upright.

"You'll have to get it out, won't you?" I said in a tight voice.

"No sweat. We've all done field surgery. Even on colonels. Right, Major?"

"Right," the major's deeper voice assured me. His hand pressed comfortingly against my waist. "Merlin had him by the arm, too, but the man in the car shot him. Shot him twice," and the major's voice turned hard and cold. "To make sure."

The lieutenant muttered under his breath. He sighed and straightened up, looking at the major.

"I'll need a good sharp knife, sterilized. Is that a field kit, Laird?"

"Yes, it's got a probe."

"Good. Hope he stays out. His teeth are sharp as I'm sure our catman found out," and the lieutenant bared his own teeth in a malicious grin. He washed his hands very carefully.

"Merlin won't bite you," I declared.

"All in a good cause," the lieutenant said lightly, using a sink brush vigorously on his nails. "Many men have survived my tender ministrations, Miss Carla, and walked away to fight again. We got him in out of the cold which could he bad for open wounds."

He dried his hands and looked critically at Merlin.

"It'll be easier on all of us if he sleeps on."

"He wouldn't bite you even if he did wake," I reasserted loyally.

"Of course not. The dog's got more sense than most humans. Here's Turtle now."

Turtle stamped in, breathing stertorously. His language, even for him, was incredible, his expressiveness therapeutic. He came right up to Merlin, glancing anxiously at the two officers. When he saw their confident expressions, he straightened up.

"Snow slowed me. They got clean away, the _____," he said curtly.

"Now, Miss Carla, you hold both lights, like so." The lieutenant positioned my hands. "I want you two to be ready to hold him. Put your full weight on him if necessary. Bailey, you lean across his shoulders, to keep his head down. Major, take his hips. His frame is strong. The important thing will be to keep him from moving while I'm probing. Ready?"

"Wouldn't more light be better?" I asked fearfully.

"This is more than we usually have," Turtle grunted.

The major held up an ampule of morphine from the field kit.

"This might help," he suggested.

"Dose isn't calibrated for a dog, damn it all." The lieutenant rejected the idea with the first swearwords I'd heard him use. He picked up the knife, a wicked-looking gleam running its sharp length in the lamplight. He took a deep preliminary breath and, with sensitive fingers, felt around the slug where it bulged slightly in the fleshy part of the shoulder.

Soon my arms, numbed by being held so high so long, began to tremble. The major took the lamps from me, leaving me standing stupidly useless.

The bullet had creased Merlin's head between his ears. A little lower and it would have entered the brain. For a wild shot on a dark night it had been all too close! I turned quickly to the counter and fumbled along it for the half-filled glass of whiskey. I took a deep swallow.

"There," said the lieutenant's voice, full of relief for the task accomplished. "That'll fix him. I wonder, do dogs get headaches? By rights, he'll have a beauty."

"Thanks," I said in so low a voice I wondered if anyone could hear me. "Thanks," I croaked again only this time my voice sounded too loud and very unsteady.

Two hands closed firmly around my shoulders. I thought for one moment it was the lieutenant but, as I leaned back grateful for the sympathy conveyed by the gesture, I realized it was Major Laird.

"Take another jolt, Carlysle," he murmured softly, giving me a little squeeze. I felt his hand brush my hair, half caress, half reassurance.

I obeyed and then turned around. Over Merlin's still form, the lieutenant caught my eyes. He draped a blanket loosely over the dog, his gestures quick and sure despite the strain he'd been under.

"Protecting him from shock will be the important thing. He didn't lose much blood and we got him out of the cold quickly."

DeLord skirted the table and began to wash his hands. The major and Turtle were conferring. Then Turtle left the kitchen as the major experimentally sloshed the coffeepot.

"You're very knowledgeable about animals," I said inanely to DeLord, trying to get out a phrase that might possibly express a gratitude too deeply felt to voice. I put my hand impulsively on his damp forearm, instinctively trying to communicate my sincerity by touch alone.

"Raised on a farm, Miss Carla. Bound to learn how to take care of sick and injured critters." He patted my hand understandingly.

"I can't ever thank you enough."

He shrugged. "I'd feel better if we could have a professional check that over," he sighed, glancing over at Merlin. "Sutures could be tighter."

"He hasn't come to," I said, biting my Up anxiously.

"That was a clout, bullet notwithstanding," the major remarked, putting a coffee cup in my hand. "Irish coffee," he added when he saw me looking around for my whiskey. "You got creased, DeLord. Tell Carlysle how long you were out."

Grinning with boyish ruefulness, the lieutenant's hand had flown to his head, gingerly touching the scar.

"Several hours, they do say," he replied. "Now, don't you worry," he admonished me kindly.

Turtle clumped back in with a bundle of quilts.

"Over here by the stove, sergeant," the major ordered and I watched, vestiges of outraged housewifely conscience rising to protest as valuable hand-pieced quilts were laid down as a sick-bed for my dog. Even if Mrs. Laird's ghost was turning in its grave, my estimation of the major rose.

"We don't want him falling off the table," DeLord said.

With great care the three men settled my Merlin on the quilts, covering him meticulously as if he had been a valued human buddy.

I was about to sit down beside him, preparing to be by his side the rest of the night, when the major took a firm hold on my arm, propelling me towards the study.

"Oh no you don't."

"But he'll need me;" I protested, trying to escape.

"Old Doc DeLord's volunteered for this detail," the lieutenant put in, dodging around the table to take my other arm.

I couldn't fight both of them, not that I had the strength to.

"You've been through quite enough tonight," Regan Laird continued inexorably. He seated me on his bed, throwing a spare blanket around me. "Now you'll finish your coffee and then go to bed. Sergeant, did you get the license on the truck?"

"Naw, sir. Either they covered it up or it was plain too dark. Night like tonight, I couldn't tell what color the car was but it was a Chevvie body. I'd say about 1938. I lost them by the time they reached the second turn onto the good road. Geez, I coulda sworn I'd punctured the gas tank."

The major turned expectantly to DeLord.

"Your eyesight's failing, Bailey. The truck was light gray. The burglar was about five nine, slight build, too muffled in clothing to tell much more. But he sure could move in the snow," DeLord remarked. "I think I winged the driver. I'm not sure but he gave up shooting and started cussing."

The major nodded, digesting the information.

"Driver was just a dark blob," he added and then exploded unexpectedly. "Goddamit, DeLord, where do you fit in all this?"

I was feeling all relaxed suddenly and the fact that the major hadn't guessed was extraordinarily funny.

"He's provost marshal, guardian dear. Maybe even CID."

All three men turned to me with various expressions of astonishment on their faces. I found it difficult to focus my eyes and blinked to clear my vision.

"Provost marshal?" Turtle bellowed, half rising from his chair, disbelief and desperation on his face. "CID?"

The lieutenant ducked his head, his fingers smoothing down the crease scar.

"She's right, I'm afraid."

"Course I'm ri . . . right. . . ." I was having the hardest time enunciating. "Summuns wron wi' me," and I felt myself falling sideways into darkness. The last thing I saw was the major's satisfied grin and I knew that there was more in that coffee than whiskey.

10

WHEN I WOKE the room was brilliant with sunlight reflecting off snow. I hadn't realized my windows faced due east. I lay there for a moment, logy in brain and body. I yawned fit to pop my jaw, covering my mouth belatedly. My watch registered ten and, positive it had stopped the previous night, I wound it. Then I realized Merlin was absent.

I was out of the bed in a single motion, grabbing my robe on the way to the door. The floor was icy under my bare feet as I flew down the stairs and burst into the kitchen, ignoring the three men, eyes only for Merlin in the corner.

He raised his head weakly, whining a greeting. I could see him gathering his body to rise. The pain of his wounds forced a yip out of him. I signaled him to stay, hurt to the quick that my entrance caused him the least unnecessary pain.

I fell on my knees beside him, crooning softly, stroking his muzzle and ears, kissing him, talking to him, in an excessive display of relieved affection. He licked my face, something he rarely did, and lay back with a sigh, letting me fuss over him, answering me with his own version of a croon, deep in his throat.

"He's all right," I told the world, dashing tears from my cheeks, only that moment aware I was crying with relief. "He's all right?" I questioned, turning to DeLord for confirmation.

"Fine. Drank a half gallon of water," DeLord nodded. "Very good patient. I know plenty could take lessons from this dog."

"You bet," Turtle rumbled.

"You!" I began, pointing to the major at the far end of the table. I got to my feet and marched myself over to him, for once at an advantage because he was seated. "You drugged that coffee."

"Damn well told," the major agreed. "You were out on your feet and too damned stubborn a little fool to know it—" Having delivered this considered opinion, he calmly continued to eat his breakfast.

"Flapjacks, Little Bit?" asked Turtle rising and going to the stove.

I glared at him, indecisively. The major wasn't going to let me pick a quarrel with him and neither was Turtle.

"Okay, okay," I said, not the least bit gracious, flopping into a chair. "Pull your diversionary tactics. I'll wait."

The lieutenant, with what I now realized was a habitual gesture on his part, ducked his head and smoothed the scar crease. I sighed with exasperation.

"You are all alike, all of you, and that includes my fine fourfooted friend." Merlin answered with a placating whine, raising his head from his quilt a few inches before he sighed plaintively and laid down again. I jerked my finger over my shoulder at him, tapping my foot. "Can't say anything around here."

"Sleep well?" asked the major politely, but even his mouth twitched in an effort not to laugh at my frustration.

"No fault of yours." I glared.

"Drink this and shut up," Turtle ordered, putting coffee in front of me.

"Is it safe?" I asked sarcastically.

Turtle snorted and turned to tend his flapjacks. I sipped rebelliously because I was not going to get anywhere. They had been perfectly justified and I had better adjust to it. As if he sensed my softening, the major leaned forward, touching my arm lightly, so I'd look at him.

"Do you remember identifying DeLord last night?"

I glanced, startled, at the lieutenant and then remembered. That did much to restore my battered self-esteem.

"Yes, and I was right, wasn't I?"

The lieutenant nodded.

"Well," Major Laird continued, scratching the back of his neck with his forefinger, "he told us why he was masquerading. And it is serious."

"Dad?" I cried out so sharply Merlin whined. I absently signaled him to stay down.

"No, no, your father knew about it," DeLord hastened to say. "Although to be quite candid, I had to suspect him, too."

"The stamps?" I queried, adding facts up.

The major held up his hand for me to slow down with wild guessing. The lieutenant grinned.

"She's quick."

"Let us explain the whole thing, will you, Carlysle," the major suggested patiently.

"Then Dad was murdered!"

"Car-lysle!" the major snapped in an authoritative tone.

DeLord's hand went up to interrupt the major's reprimand.

"Yes, only I didn't know that until last night. It puts another complexion on the whole situation." His fingers lightly pressed my hand. "Believe me, had we any idea that would happen, we would have acted with more dispatch. But we had only circumstantial evidence that points to the One Hundred and Fifteenth Regiment. As far as my superiors were concerned, it was serious but not an acute situation. Naturally, I could take only the colonel into my confidence when I was assigned to the case. Matter of fact," and he grinned ruefully, "the major was one of my prime suspects."

Incredulous, I stared at my guardian.

"You see, Miss Carla, it had to be someone with enough sophistication to know what to loot."

"Loot? It was looting?" I glanced at Turtle.

"Yes, looting. Not just trinkets or ghoul jobs on corpses. But items of intrinsic or tangible value. Jewels, stamps as you suggested, even some rare letters and a rare and immeasurably valuable Book of the Hours. Very old, more than priceless to its custodian. These are things an educated man would know to steal."

"But why was my father murdered?"

"Your father had identified the thief . . . to his satisfaction. He was obviously murdered to keep from disclosing what he knew."

"For a mess of jewelry and stamps?" I cried, appalled at the horrible, horrible wastefulness.

The lieutenant shook his head slowly from side to side.

"I'm afraid it was more than a mess of jewelry and stamps. The estimated value of the losses is close to several hundred thousand dollars."

I stared in silence at the lieutenant.

"It took us some time to narrow down our search when the initial reports came in after the Falaise-Argentan pocket was wiped out. There were items stolen by the German Seventh Army that should have been recovered in their baggage vans and weren't. I was detached from CAO to the MF Double A S . . ."

"The what?" I asked.

"The Monuments, Fine Arts and Archives Section. So the French wouldn't find their art treasures on a quick trip overseas to America. All soldiers are light-fingered. Then we found ourselves with too many potential masterminds." The lieutenant stroked his head but he didn't smile. "When your father and I crossed paths in Paris that time, I eliminated him completely. I asked him to request a replacement and I'd make sure it was me. Then I could work directly in the regiment without being suspected. We checked everyone. Including you, Major."

The major was frowning in concentration and suddenly his face cleared. He pointed directly at the lieutenant, snapping his fingers as his thoughts crystallized.

"That lecture on autographs! Bonaparte, Louis, ye gods. I thought you'd gone into battle shock. We were at the assembly area at Montcarnet, right?"

The lieutenant nodded. Regan Laird's face clouded again, the muscles tightened along his jaw, and his eyes turned bleak.

"That leaves us with . . ."

"That's right, Laird,"

"Warren!" I exploded out of my chair. "Warren killed my father."

"We believe so," DeLord said quietly.

"Believe so?" I echoed, aggravated at his calmness.

He sighed. "Believe me, I sympathize, Miss Carla. Unfortunately, although my earnest private desire is to arrest Warren immediately—"

"But weren't you and Dad on the way to arrest Warren the night he murdered Dad?"

DeLord shook his head. "Your father had laid a trap for the looter with several valuable stamps and some jeweled crosses. We had to find them in the thief's possession, you know, to press charges. Frankly, I hadn't suspected Warren. I had my eye on one of the Third Battalion smart operators. I thought at the time your father was going to order Warren back to HO. He should've after that stunt with the beetfields!" The lieutenant's face was grim. "Now I know why, against all logic, your father had to keep Warren on the line.

"Fer Chrissake!" Turtle growled softly.

"So after your father . . . died, I had to go on alone, set up another trap which also meant the necessity of—"

"Sucking up to Warren?" Turtle interrupted again, his eyes narrowing.

DeLord nodded. "The bait was taken and then I couldn' find it!" He grimaced with distaste and dismay. "And that was the hardest blow. It has to be Warren because he was the last person to handle the items. But he didn't have them and I searched, believe me, I searched. I even drugged his coffee one night to search him personally. And I had to find out how he disposed of the loot. There were some mighty valuable pieces; involved by then and they've got to be recovered."

"And my father's murder is less important than—"

"No, no," DeLord hastily interrupted, his eyes shocked at that suggestion. "But l didn't know that until last night. Now the serial number has been filed off that Colt but I think we can get enough to reconstruct it and trace the issue. Unfortunately, Miss Carla, we have to have proof to bring an officer to court- martial. Proof of murder and proof of grand larceny."

"But I'm no longer army," I said through my gritted teeth,

"and I don't need any further proof. Warren's waiting for me in Boston."

I swung my chair around, grabbing for the pile of letters on the sideboard. The major caught my arm as I passed him and jerked me sharply to my feet. I tried to twist free but he was on his feet, hands on my shoulders, shaking me hard.

"But I'm not having my ward up for murder. Now you stop this ranting around . . . right now. . . ." He gave me a neck-snapping shake, bruising my shoulders with his powerful hands. "You're army as long as I'm your guardian. Just remember that, Carlysle. And I give the orders. I expect them to be obeyed."

He forced my chin up, his eyes glinting angrily down at me.

"You don't go off half-cocked into a battle if you want to win it." Again he shook me but not so hard, because I knew he was right and he sensed it. "You want Warren? Not half as bad as DeLord, Bailey, I and the U.S. Army want him. And you're going to help get him because, my dear ward, you're the new bait. Someone tried to burgle this house last night. Two attempts . . . no three, were made in Cambridge. Now sit down and listen."

He gave me a little push and I stumbled back into my chair, rubbing my shoulders absently.

"We think he's after the gun. DeLord thinks he might be after more than that. . . ."

Merlin interrupted with a bark. His head was turned towards the front of the house and his manner, despite his weakened condition, was alert. He barked again with more strength and struggled to rise.

Turtle was halfway through the corridor before I could force Merlin down. The open door gave a clear view of the front windows and the police car that slid sideways on the snow to a stop in front of the house.

"The shots last night?" DeLord asked.

"The burglary at Mrs. Everett's," I countered flatly.

Merlin growled, an angry frustrated snarl of a growl. His head slewed around to the rear of the house. I grabbed at the major's arm, pointing.

"We're surrounded," I cried out, for a navy patrol, led by two Dobermans straining on their leashes, came tramping out of the scrub at the rear of the house.

"Those shots!" the major said conclusively.

"Christ! Shore Patrol!" Turtle grated out. Two blue jeeps had drawn up beside the police car and armed men were piling out of all three cars.

The policeman gesticulating at the house was cut off bluntly by a gesture from the SP officer. Just then Turtle yanked open the door.

"Whaddya want?"

And the second patrol banged on the back door.

I fell on Merlin to keep him down. DeLord came to my assistance as the major, his face set, went to deal with the rear assault group.

"Let's see your papers, Major," a stern voice ordered Laird through Merlin's snarls.

The Dobermans, aware of another dog's presence, set up a deafening hullabaloo. I heard a noisy scrambling over the incensed barking and the back door was slammed, cutting the canine chorus down appreciably.

"This is all snafu." DeLord grinned at me over Merlin's writhing body.

"Goddamitall, Merlin, at ease!" I ordered, slapping his muzzle in my desperation to keep him from opening his wounds. He whined piteously at the unexpectedly severe reprimand. With an aggressive expression in his eyes, he had to content himself with growling at the Dobermans who were still roaring outside.

"Come in, Ensign," Laird was saying. "May I inquire why my house has been surrounded?"

"Your papers, Major!" the shore patrolman repeated flintily. The man had entered the back hall far enough to see the lieutenant and me sprawled over Merlin's body. He stared at us, turning slightly to expose the drawn thirty-eight in his hand.

"Shut your dogs up, Ensign," I cried. "Mine's been wounded and I've got to keep him quiet." With those Dobermans sounding off, Merlin would not relax.

"Ensign, I'm Lieutenant Robert DeLord, Provost Marshall, on special assignment with Major Laird and Sergeant Bailey." The authority in his voice was incongruous with his semirecumbent position.

The coastguardsman had to crouch to see the lieutenant.

"If you'll muzzle your dogs, I can get up and show you my identification."

"Belay those dogs, mister!" the ensign bellowed, his volume equal to Turtle's parade voice. The Dobermans were silenced.

At this point, Turtle stomped back into the kitchen, his face black with indignant anger. A police officer and another shore patrol j.g. followed him. I could see two men taking positions at the front door. One carried a tommy gun at the ready.

"You get up, Merlin, and I'll whip you. Whip you. Hear?" I muttered savagely before I scrambled to my feet. Cold air swirled around my bare toes.

"Close that door!" I cried.

"Chrissake, Lieutenant, they think we're Nazis, landed by sub last night!" announced Turtle at the top of his lungs, his Dorchester accent unmistakable. No Nazi was that good an imitator.

Laird was now showing the ensign his orders. The sandpeep's manners thawed considerably.

"Thank you, sir. Lieutenant?" and the ensign took the major's papers over to his j.g.

The kitchen, large enough for many, seemed awfully crowded with armed and angry men.

"These look all right," the j.g. remarked dubiously, passing them on to the policeman who waved them aside. He had been staring in an unpleasant way at the major.

"Eyah. I know Laird."

At the curiously antagonistic comment, Regan Laird turned his face slightly to the left so that his good profile was in full view of the policeman. The man nodded coldly.

"Eyah, that's Regan Laird."

"Beatty," the major said by way of greeting.

"Who are these others, then?" demanded the j.g.

The policeman lifted heavy shoulders in a shrug.

"I'll vouch for them," the major said quickly. "Both the sergeant and the lieutenant served with me in the Fifth Corps."

"The lieutenant says he's provost marshal," the ensign tacked on.

DeLord bore the keen scrutiny, with poise.

"Know about the shooting last night?" the shore patrolman asked.

"Yes." DeLord's flat answer was intended to discourage further questions.

"I have to ask for an explanation, lieutenant," the j.g. insisted, shifting his weight.

"Will you tell them to shut that front door?" I hissed, seizing my opportunity.

"Who are you?" the policeman asked.

"I'm James Carlysle Murdock," I said, with a grimace, steeling myself for the inevitable reaction.

"My ward," the major inserted. "The daughter of my commanding officer who was killed in Europe."

Questions were effectively silenced and the intruders shuffled nervously. I saw the j.g. give a signal and I heard the door close.

The policeman was looking at me speculatively now.

"I want to know about those shots, too," he asserted, looking from me to the major. Laird gestured to DeLord.

I made a quick bet with myself, and won. DeLord ducked his head and fingered his scar.

"We had an unexpected visitor last night," the lieutenant said, having gathered his thoughts together. "Naturally we took off after him. So did the dog and when the burglar's accomplice took a shot at Merlin, well, naturally we took defensive action."

"Did it occur to you that you would alarm the coast with such unauthorized gunfire?" the j.g. snapped in an acid voice. "Don't you guys know there's a. . . ." He stopped. He had the decency to look abashed as his eyes darted to the major's ruined face. His own countenance turned bright red with embarrassment. Turtle's surly growl indicated his opinion of the navy.

"No, I'm afraid it didn't," DeLord replied with more humility than I'd have used under the circumstances. "For one thing," and I couldn't see why he felt he had to justify our actions, "Miss Murdock's dog was seriously wounded. For another, we have no way of communicating with the authorities."

"Well," the j.g. grumbled, "this isn't our jurisdiction at all then." He saluted the major, jerked his head significantly at the ensign in lieu of an order. The front-door party of patrolmen withdrew with what I considered rather bad grace since we were not at fault.

"A moment, Ensign," DeLord said after Turtle closed the hall door on the first group. "Any of your men trained in veterinary skills? I'd appreciate someone looking at the shepherd."

"Sure, Lieutenant, just a minute." The ensign was not at all disgruntled.

"That can wait," said the policeman officiously. "I've a few questions."

"They've waited this long, they can wait a little longer," I retorted, glaring at him.

He turned his head in my direction slowly and gave me a long look, compounded of annoyance that I had spoken in the first place, then insolence as he realized I was older than I looked.

"It won't take a moment," the lieutenant assured Beatty diplomatically.

I began not to like this young man suddenly.

Beatty ignored the lieutenant, pulling a slip of paper out of his pocket. He consulted it for a moment.

"I've been asked by the Cambridge police to question a James Carlysle Murdock concerning a burglary in her boardinghouse room . . . Burglary! And you had one last night, too? What in hell's going on here?" and he glared around menacingly.

The ensign returned with a sailor who pushed past the major with a polite excuse and suppressed curiosity.

"Evans has had some training, miss," the ensign said and we all stepped aside for the sailor to look at Merlin.

"Merlin! Friend," I told the dog as Evans, his face lighting with admiration for the shepherd, bent slowly, his hand extended.

Merlin whined, licked his lips, but let the sailor examine his head.

"That's a bad crease, miss, but it's clean."

"We dug a bullet out of his shoulder," the lieutenant said.

Evans turned back the quilt and whistled. I heard him pull in his breath sharply as he saw the wound. He put the quilt back and stood up.

"That's beyond me, sir. And he's too good a dog not to have the best."

Evans turned to me, his face eager. "Ever thought of donating him to the K-9 Corps?"

Turtle snorted. I held up a warning hand.

"He's been in, sailor," I said gravely.

I know it was outrageous to imply that Merlin had seen service and been retired honorably but I didn't want him belittled any further with explanations after his heroism of the night before.

Evan's eyes widened and he saluted.

"There's a good vet in Hyannis, miss. With the ensign's permission, I'll give him a call. He'll come out if I say so."

"We'd appreciate it, sailor," the major said smoothly, moving to my side, his manner, for some reason, protective. I glanced up at him inquiringly and caught, out of the side of my vision, the smirk on Beatty's face. I didn't like it.

"Thank you, Evans," I said, not to let the major do the honors for me exclusively.

The Coast Guard contingent left with expressions of apology and good will. Merlin growled low in his throat as the Dobermans' baying announced withdrawal.

"All right, now," Beatty said. He pulled a chair from the table and sat himself down, opening his heavy coat, taking out report forms, and a pen, his long, lantern-jawed, mulish face disagreeable.

"I want a few things cleared up on the civilian level," he said nastily.

I saw the lieutenant ease himself out to the study.

"There's been some hanky-panky heyah that I don't miss even if you pulled rank and all on them sandpeeps."

"I'm sorry, officer," the lieutenant said smoothly. He held out to the policeman a small leather case and a folded sheet of army issue paper. "This matter is now classified."

"What in hell you say?" He reluctantly took the papers from DeLord. His eyes widened with outraged surprise. "I don't believe it. Burglaries? Classified?"

"I'm working out of Fort Edwards at the moment. Call CID for verification. This is my code number."

I began to like the lieutenant again.

"I don't like it," Beatty said flatly. He thrust the chair back angrily as he rose. "I don't like it one bit." He waved a finger under DeLord's nose, his anger growing with each shake. "And don't think for one moment, Lieutenant, that I'm not going to call Edwards. There's something godalmighty fishy about this. Burglaries! Shooting!" He turned to include me in his catalog. "Wards! Hell. I know you too well, Regan Laird."

"Now, wait a minute," Turtle growled, placing himself belligerently in Beatty's path. "You don't—"

"You look familiar, Sergeant," Beatty interrupted him pugnaciously, his lantern jaw jutting out. "You at Edwards?"

"Bailey's just back from Germany," Laird intervened. At his stern look, Turtle stood aside as Beatty, casting one more meaningful sneer over his shoulder, stalked out the door. Merlin's soft snarl summed up my feelings exactly.

"I don't think we've seen the last of him," the lieutenant remarked ruefully, his hand reaching for his head.

"Leave that damn thing alone," I snapped with irritation, pulling a chair near the stove and curling my cold feet under me.

"Edwards does know?" the major asked hopefully.

"Oh, indeed, they do," DeLord replied. "You know this Beatty fellow?"

The major sat down heavily, lighting a cigarette and inhaling deeply before he answered. "Beatty and I have had a few run-ins before."

"Speeding?" I taunted flippantly.

The major shook his head. "Long before I started driving, Carlysle, and long before he got on the force. I came here for summers as a child, you know."

"No, I didn't know," I said caustically.

He ignored me. "If my memory serves me correctly, the initial engagement was fought over some crabs."

"Crabs?" Turtle exploded. Merlin barked.

"Crabs," the major reaffirmed, amusement lighting his face. The lieutenant began to chuckle. "I believe we were about ten at the time. I lost all the crabs I'd caught—a whole morning's work—and came home without the net and with a black eye."

"And Beatty?" I prompted hopefully.

"Oh, he was crabless, too, and minus a front tooth."

"And you're still fighting over that?"

"No," Laird allowed, setting his jaw against what he had no intention of discussing. "There were a few other . . . minor . . . disagreements."

Turtle chuckled understandingly and had that special look which I had learned meant members of my sex were involved.

"However," and the major's attitude changed abruptly as he turned to me, "it only points up my reasons for wanting you out of here."

"That?" I exclaimed, gesturing at the door where Beatty had exited.

"That!" Laird repeated emphatically. "I don't trust Beatty's discretion any further than I can throw him. And I would if it'd serve any purpose. It's going to be all over Orleans that I have a good-looking adolescent ward—"

"I am not adolescent," I objected strenuously. I did not fail to catch the other adjective and treasured it.

"Shut up. And that's going to ruin your reputation."

"But Turtle and the lieutenant are here . . ."

"Turtle possibly constitutes a chaperon but the lieutenant? Sorry, Mrs. Grundy says no."

"A backhanded compliment if ever I had one." DeLord chuckled and then hastened, spurred by Major Laird's angry look, to add his weight to the argument. "But the major's right, Miss Carla. Beatty is no gentleman."

"Now, wait a minute," I suggested, my dander rising on several fronts, "there's one helluva lot more at stake than my reputation. About which I'm not worried." I glared at all of them impartially. "Have you so easily forgotten my father's murder? You started to outline what we were going to do next to trap Warren. And I warn you, all of you, I'm not giving up that little item. I want Warren up for court-martial, you, the major, the shore patrol, Beatty, and the entire town of Orleans notwithstanding." I looked at each man belligerently, knowing I had a very strong case.

"Furthermore, Merlin can't be moved. And if I'm not here, he plain won't eat. You're not going to sacrifice him to convention, are you? Because I won't."

"That C.G. rating said he'd call the vet," the major said evasively. "Maybe he can be moved."

"Over snowy roads, in a jeep?" I asked sarcastically. "Ever done it, wounded?" and bit my lip because the look on Turtle's face, not to mention the major's, gave me a definitive answer to that. I swallowed and changed my tactics. "That burglar last night wasn't Warren because Donald Warren would have frozen solid with fright if Merlin were anywhere near him. But I'll bet Warren hired him."

"How would Warren know where you were?" the major countered.

"Ahh," I cried in exasperation. "He wrote me at the Cambridge address, didn't he? He was to be in Boston the twenty-eighth, he and his precious Marian. One quick phone call to Mrs. Everett to arrange a state visit from Lieutenant Colonel and Mrs. Donald Warren, sweetly simpering, sympathetic, solicitous . . . sickening!" I waved my hands, erasing the scene. "And Mrs. Everett who is a sweet lady is not very bright. 'Oh, I'm so sorry. But she's staying with her guardian on Cape Cod,'" and I mimicked the Dorchester accent. "Sure they know where I am. And you may be damned sure they didn't tell their second-story man my dog was here, particularly if it's the same thug who tried to burgle Mrs. Everett's."

"Which brings up another point," the lieutenant interrupted. "I'd like your permission to go through your father's footlocker, Miss Carla."

"Of course. We've been theorizing entirely too much."

"Get dressed first, Carlysle," the major ordered as I led the way upstairs.

I got as far as the door to the little back room before Regan Laird caught up with me. He picked me up bodily and turned me around. He marched me back to my bedroom and thrust me inside. The room was frigid as I'd left the door open.

"It's freezing in here," I complained as he shut me in.

"Too bad. Teach you to shut doors in the future. But you don't leave that room until you're warmly dressed."

"I want to be there when—"

"We won't touch your father's things till you're present," he snapped. "Now dress. On the double."

11

WITH FINGERS which fumbled from cold and frustration, I threw on clothes, stamped into boots, and threw open the door. The major was leaning against the jamb, a pleased expression on his face. I could have slapped him.

"Better put a few logs on the fire while you're at it. Warm the room up for later."

I glared at him, tapped my foot and, seeing my irritation only amused him further, I whirled and slammed some logs on the grate. Of course, then I had to sweep up the scattered coals and clinkers.

"Haste makes waste," he chanted from the door.

I raised the fire tongs menacingly and gasped as he instinctively crouched. He strode across the room, his eyes flashing, and jerked the tongs out of my hand.

"That's just enough of that, young lady." He gripped me at the elbows and gave me a hard shake. "I've put up with your bad temper, your moodiness, your insolence because I've been sorry for you. Honestly sorry. But enough is enough. You keep that temper under control or I'll turn you over my knee. Do I make myself clear?"

I was scared of him. And ashamed of myself. I lowered my eyes and swallowed hard.

"I'm truly sorry, Major. I've behaved abominably and I do apologize."

He gave me another little shake, accepting my penitence.

"All right then. Your father saw fit, God knows why, to make me your guardian. As you say, you're nearly twenty-one so our association will be brief. I'd rather it was as pleasant as possible because it is my intention to discharge my duties to the best of my ability. In spite of you."

I still couldn't look at him. He was absolutely right. I had been a self-centered, childish, irresponsible brat. He drew in a deep breath and let it out in a rush, holding out his right hand.

"Now, let's call a truce."

I put my hand gratefully in his and he covered it with his left, pressing it in a friendly way. Then he tipped my face up so I had to look him in the eye. He regarded me seriously for a moment and then smiled slowly.

"You've got pretty eyes, brat," as if he had just noticed I had eyes at all.

He put one arm around my shoulders companionably and led me downstairs.

Turtle and DeLord had cleared the kitchen table and placed the army locker on it. We went through the footlocker, and the lieutenant and I checked through the three albums carefully.

"There's nothing in here. I don't see stamps that are particularly valuable," I said.

The major who had watched for a while decided to make coffee. As he opened the canister he started to swear.

"That tears it. No coffee. Okay, ration stamps everybody."

Turtle flushed. "Left mine with my sister-in-law, Major. Didn't expect to be here so long."

"I've some," the lieutenant said.

"Mine are upstairs but you don't need stamps for coffee," I exclaimed, turning back at the door.

"I need them for meat and sugar, Carlysle. And I'm not making a trip into Orleans for just coffee. I didn't plan on so many guests." His grin belied any inhospitality.

I dashed upstairs for my ration cards, throwing aside last night's disordered clothing as I rummaged through my suitcase for the folder. My hand crumpled some paper. I remembered the two sheets in the German album. I retrieved the lists, jubilant. They must mean something and possibly DeLord would know. I did remember to snatch up the ration books and came triumphantly back downstairs.

"I've got something," I babbled, pressing the ration books in the major's hand for he was all dressed to leave. I waved the sheets in DeLord's face, crowing in triumph.

"At ease, at ease," laughed the lieutenant, unable to see why I was excited.

"If I don't get started now, I'll never go," the major said. "Explain it to me later."

"Go, go, go," I crowed as the lieutenant took the sheets from me, frowning at first and then beginning to smile.

"This is it. These are the lists of the first trap your father set. The reason I was in Paris and doing the rounds of the stamp merchants was to see if some valuable stamps and old books known to have been appropriated by four high-ranking German officers had turned up yet," DeLord said. "I ran into your father in a little store near the Plaza Athenee. You can imagine my surprise at seeing someone from the suspected regiment in a stamp shop." DeLord rolled his eyes expressively. "It didn't take me very long to realize your father was not the looter."

"I should hope so."

"Well, remember, he had both the knowledge and the opportunity. Now, these particular stamps and the rare illuminated books should have been 'liberated' when we erased the Falaise-Argentan retreat alley the Germans managed to keep open so long. A lot of kraut baggage transports were captured and the stuff should have turned up. And the unit which came on the transports first was the One Hundred and Fifteenth."

"Yeah," and Turtle looked off into the middle distance, remembering. "Yeah. That figgers. I remember."

"It does figger, doesn't it?" DeLord agreed gravely, "and the Third Battalion overtook that train, too."

Turtle continued to nod as though more pieces of the puzzle were fitting together.

"Yeah, I'm remembering a lot now," and his face twisted into an ugly expression of distaste. "Yeah. And Major Warren was so set on inspections to keep looting down to a minimum in his regiment. He even snafued me with a. . . ." He stopped as he caught the lieutenant's glance. "Christ, Lieutenant, spoils of war! But, when I think of the angle that lousy bastard worked, so high and righteous. . . ." He pulled his head between his shoulders belligerently and cracked his knuckles sharply as if he wished they were Warren's neckbones. "Yeah, he knew well we wouldn't question him! And part of it is, we didn't. We thought that bastard turned everything over to regimental when they came around on pickup." Turtle's laugh was ugly. "Christ, but I'm glad I. . . ." and he broke off, blinking, and looked around at me with a basilisk stare.

I don't know what he intended to say but I know he felt he had said too much already. The lieutenant had not been paying attention for he had been deep in his own ruminations. He slapped the sheet he held.

"Help me with this list, Miss Carla. Those stamps must be somewhere in this locker. Bailey, remember when you caught the colonel coming in from a recon near Baesweiler?"

Turtle nodded.

"Well, we'd just planted the stamps on an abandoned baggage lorry which Recon had spotted on an aerial sweep. The colonel planned to do a thorough search of anyone who got near it. I thought the trap had failed because I remember Warren pulled a search before we could. And he made such an issue of sending the stuff back to HQ. The call that Colonel Murdock got just as he ordered me to go get Warren was to tell him that the planted bait had not reappeared at HQ. He called me back and we both went to get Warren. Only, at the time, I thought the colonel had finally made up his mind to transfer Warren out of the line. And, of course, we never got to Warren."

Turtle cursed under his breath.

I bent hastily over the German album, straightening a stamp in its treads. This particular album was made with strips to retain the stamps in place without gummed tabs. As I fooled needlessly to cover my inner pain, I pushed it to one side and . . . disclosed the stamp carefully inserted behind it. The second stamp was not a duplicate. Furthermore it was one of the violet-orange 75-centimes French-Chinese stamps and as valuable as it could be! The 75-centimes was inverted! Information was triggered in my mind and I didn't need any Scott to remind me this little piece of pretty paper was worth several thousand dollars. In fact, the French at that time seemed to have a problem with the 75-centimes stamps all along the line and the inversions were as valuable as they were rare.

"Look!" I gabbled excitedly. "Here's our proof. Here's one of them. See, the seventy-five centimes is inverted. They're priceless. All by themselves." I had difficulty keeping my fingers careful as I discovered more of the rare inversions. And, sure enough, amid some perfectly unexceptional French Egyptian stamps were some of the valuable carmine and purple hand stamped Tchongking of 1900.

"Gawd," I exclaimed, spreading the finds out delicately on the table for them all to see, "Dad must've just died to find these. Oh!" I closed my eyes against the pain of that imbecilic idiom.

"What are these paper-wrapped packages?" DeLord asked evenly.

I forced myself to see what he held. "I haven't looked yet."

The lieutenant undid the string. Pushing back the paper, he whistled in amazement. I glanced up and my eyes widened with surprise. That was no album.

"What in hell's that?" Tittle growled.

Reverently, the lieutenant opened the heavy tooled cover, exposing the first illuminated sheet with its elaborate and beautiful titles, red, black, and gold. Even the borders were in gold. There were about eighteen or so lines, arranged in one column on the back, framed by those magnificently intricate, monk-conceived borders.

"*Confessio Santa Fulgentii . . .*" the lieutenant read hesitantly as he deciphered the ancient script. He whistled again, carefully turning the next page of heavy but brittle-looking vellum. Some of the gold in the border on this page had faded and the green background showed through.

"That's one of those Books of Hours or something," I said in an awed voice.

"No wonder the MFAAC had me assigned to find out what was happening." The lieutenant's eyes were wide. "This thing is priceless."

"Can't even read it," Turtle remarked dourly.

There were two other wrapped packages which we lifted out with great reverence. One was quite small but rather thick for the leaves were heavy vellum. The illumination was even more elaborate than the "Confession," " purple bands, gold lettering, the most intricate initials and borders. Pictures in many colors with silvery borders. Just beautiful and so old, so lovingly, meticulously crafted. The lieutenant and I decided it must be the Gospels, although between the unfamiliar calligraphy and our rusty Latin it was difficult to tell.

The third was unquestionably a Bible, two columns of the black Latin script on each page. The capitals were gold and red, the titles daintier in design than the others. Lots of vines in the borders and much gold with more varied colors than the other two had boasted so the effect was more brilliant.

When I learned later what they actually were, I felt I had blasphemed even to gaze at them. The last one was an eighth or ninth century book of Gospels, stolen from the Bibliotheque de Tours. It had been used when the monarchs of France took their oaths as honorary canons of St. Martins. The smallest one was also dated in the ninth century and also Gospels, but a bedside copy.

The "Confessio" was, again, ninth century, done at St. Germain des Pres. I guess it was the brilliant golds and colors that attracted Warren and made him think they were valuable. They were but he could never have sold them. The Germans, of course, hadn't worried about selling them. They just wanted to have them.

"Those things look like money," Turtle remarked after we had carefully rewrapped the old books and put them back on the footlocker. "But these things?" and he picked up one of the "trap" stamps, a 75-centimes inverted.

"They're a fine investment," DeLord assured him, collect-

ing the squares carefully. As he reached for a transparent envelope his leg brushed against one of the cartridge boxes we had
put to one side. It fell and the sound it made striking the floor
drew our attention.

Fascinated I stared down. One of the shells had lost its lead
tip and two gemstones winked up at me.

"Chrissake!" Turtle gasped.

We grabbed up the shells and when we had finished opening them, a glittering assortment of jewels lay before us. The
second box, apparently not even sealed, contained heavy gold
and gem-encrusted crosses of ancient design.

"Will ya look at that!" Turtle said as we lined up the impressive array of wealth.

The lieutenant was shaking his head slowly from side to
side.

"The man was clever. I'll give him that. We've been looking
for these since the Cotentin. They're why PM assigned me to
the case. Tell me, Miss Carla, let's suppose Warren did call on
you. Did bring up the subject of the footlocker. I suppose he
could have inquired whether you got your father's things back
safely. He might even have inquired what was returned. Would
you have been likely to turn over to him the gun and the cartridge boxes?"

"Well," I said with a heavy sigh, "probably—yes. You're not
supposed to keep a service Colt and he'd know I know it. Yes, I
probably would have handed him over a fortune in gems and
the gun that killed my own father."

Pure hatred flooded me.

"But those books? How would he have got them back?"

DeLord grinned at me. "I only just found that out myself.
Let me backtrack a bit to where we left off before the navy
landed. What had puzzled us was how the missing valuables
were getting out of Europe. Even when I knew that Warren was
the only possible suspect, and I didn't know that until I'd
planted my own trap, I still didn't know how. I felt I was close to
the solution when the colonel got wounded at Aachen."

Turtle's laugh was very unpleasant.

"I told my superiors my suspicions and a very close check was kept on Warren's movements, contacts, and mail, while he was recuperating in the hospital. We arranged to have him transferred stateside, knowing he would have to lead us to the loot eventually if he was to realize any profit. By then, one or two items had turned up in pawnshops and in respectable antique shops. When Warren inquired when the next shipment of casualties' effects was being made, we had our first real break. He tried to arrange his passage on the same ship but we switched him to another at the last moment." DeLord's eyes danced maliciously.

"But, wait a minute, Dad's footlocker came in four weeks ago and Warren wrote me only on the twenty-sixth."

"Ah," the lieutenant said, "but when was your first burglary?"

"Oh," and there my theory blew up in my face. "About two days after it arrived. But I was in the hospital. What if I had gone through it. . . ."

"Did you?" asked the lieutenant quietly.

"I couldn't bear to."

"Exactly. And I'm sure Warren counted on this. Shock alone would keep you from examining it very closely."

"Wait a minute, you mean you knew something must be among my father's things?"

DeLord shook his head. "Not exactly, but your father's footlocker, being a colonel's and being his, would not be inspected closely, if at all. Remember, even the gun was at the bottom. The albums, the legitimate ones, were carefully on top of the illegal bibles. It wasn't until I realized that Warren, in addition 'to keeping the looting down,' also handled the effects of the fatalities that I knew how he was getting things out. Then I had to find out how he recovered them."

"Chrissake, and the colonel put him into Headquarters Company to keep him out of trouble."

"Hmmm," and DeLord hurried on. "After Julich I realized

he added things to packs. This meant someone had to intercept on this side."

"Marian Warren," I exclaimed. "You know, I thought it was awful strange that she'd bother to call on those families in the Boston area. Do you mean she was picking up loot? How would she know? How did she do it?"

"Well, we started intercepting letters from him to his wife or anyone else he wrote."

"You mean he told that harpy right out. . . ."

"Oh, no, he was discreet enough. Just suggested she go visit so-and-so's family. He had a code worked out, too, because we noticed he'd use several phrases over and over. 'He was a fine soldier,' 'he died bravely,' and 'I shall miss his leadership qualities.' When the provost marshall over here got with it and did some checking, they tracked down quite a pack smuggled through. The really valuable items, a few fine rings, a silver communion chalice dating from the fifteenth century, some very rare stamps, all came in officers' packs. They also connected several burglaries with the arrival of footlockers. Nothing had been disturbed in the house, nothing apparently was missing. But there had been burglaries just after shipments."

"'Miss his leadership' . . ." I gasped in outrage. "But . . . he said in his letter to me something about Dad's ability to command. Ye gods."

"Repeats himself, doesn't he." DeLord chuckled. "At any rate, we have it pretty well lined out now; opportunity, motive, modus operandi, but we haven't caught him with the goods and we have to or our case won't stand up."

"And why not?" I demanded indignantly. "He murdered to protect his racket."

DeLord shook his head patiently. "Circumstantial although we know now he had a motive for killing your father but, Miss Carla, until last night I didn't know your father had been murdered." He shot a significant look at Turtle.

Turtle's face drained of blood and he spun away to the stove to pour himself a cup of coffee.

"All I was out to catch was a thief who was causing some bad feelings with our allies." DeLord's voice dropped to a quiet sad tone.

I sighed deeply, shook off my apathy.

"All right, why don't you take the jeep when the major gets back and get that gun traced?"

DeLord nodded. "I've the slug that murdered your father, too," and he touched his breast pocket briefly. "I'll run a ballistics check on it as well. We'll maybe have conclusive proof."

"You mean I can't help trap Warren?" I felt cheated.

Merlin growled at that point and we turned to look at him. He continued growling, his head cocked towards the front of the house.

"Now what?" Turtle demanded wearily. "The Marines?"

"No," I cried, jumping up with relief "The vet the gob promised."

I raced to the front door, vowing to think more kindly of the Coast Guard from now on. I pulled the door open and stopped. Two cars had pulled up. One of them was an army jeep, an officer and two burly MPs filing out. The other car was Beatty's and there was a self-satisfied expression on his face as he plowed back up the swath he had cut through the snow that morning.

"What's on your mind?" I snapped.

"You'll find out soon enough, Miss Murdock," and he made the formal title an insult. His voice, brash and loud, reached Turtle's ears.

Before I realized what it was all about Beatty had pushed me roughly back and waved in the two MPs who entered, revolvers drawn.

"There's your man!" and he pointed straight at Turtle.

Turtle went into an instinctive crouch. I think he would have tried to make it out through the kitchen but, unwittingly, the lieutenant stepped into the doorway, blocking his retreat. Turtle straightened. The MP lieutenant came up to him.

"Name, rank and serial number," he asked formally.

Turtle rattled them off, defeat written in his posture.

"You're to accompany me to Camp Edwards, Sergeant."

"For the attempted murder of Lt. Col. Donald Warren," sneered Beatty.

Someone screamed and it must have been me as I ducked around Beatty and flew to Turtle, my arms around him in a futile effort to protect him.

"You can't, you can't. He served my father for twenty-eight years!"

"Sorry, miss."

"Here's the AWOL list," Beatty offered too helpfully. "Resisted arrest at Aachen and disappeared. Only they thought he was still in Europe. I never forget a face."

"May I see it?" DeLord's voice, steely and authoritative, cut across Beatty's abusive triumph.

" You can't arrest him. You can't. You've got to prove it," I screamed.

"Bit, knock it off," said Turtle, disengaging my arms from his neck.

I looked at him. I read the truth which I had before only happily suspected. He had shot Warren. But Warren had deserved to die. Warren had killed my father. It was too damned bad Turtle had missed.

"Thank you," DeLord said, his face grim as he returned the incriminating sheet to the smug policeman. "If you've no objection," and DeLord flashed his own identification, "I'd like to accompany Sergeant Bailey. I have evidence to present." His hand brushed his breast pocket.

"As you wish, DeLord," the MP said. "Get your things, Sergeant."

I had to watch as they stood over my Turtle Edward Bailey while he shrugged into his outer clothes. I had to witness the gloating expression on Beatty's face. Why did he have to show up at all, with his petty informer's nature and goddamned good memory? I had no conscience about the moralities involved in Turtle playing executioner. I was only sorry Turtle had failed.

My horror was that Turtle might have to pay too dearly for that rough disposition of justice.

It was intolerable to watch Beatty delighting in the scene. I stalked over to him stiffly.

"You get out of here, you hear me."

He glanced down at me, as if surprised I dared approach him at all.

"I'm talking to you, Beatty. You have no warrant to enter this house and no business in it. Now get yourself out of here or I'll call my dog on you for trespassing."

"Your dog's too sick to move," he sneered, slowly, insultingly.

"I'm not," DeLord said, moving me gently to one side, facing Beatty. His body was poised lightly on his toes and in his hands he held the holstered forty-five Colt. Beatty would have no way of knowing it was unloaded but he would appreciate that DeLord was in a fighting mood. "Miss Carla asked you to leave and if you do not leave. . . ." He did not complete the threat.

Beatty shot a hurried glance behind Robert DeLord. What he evidently saw in the faces of the MPs was enough to know that they would not support him. They had come for their prisoner on his information but they didn't think very much of Police Officer Beatty.

Beatty backed out of the house, his angry eyes and set lantern jaw boding no good for me. I didn't care.

Turtle was ready and he was marched out of the house, eyes front. Beatty stood to one side of the stoop to watch Turtle positioned between the two MPs in the back of the jeep. DeLord gripped my arm, gave me a reassuring squeeze.

"I'll be back as soon as I can. I've got some talking to do to Colonel Calderone. Tell Laird I'll see about the gun's issue, too." The lieutenant squinted down the road anxiously. "He ought to be back soon. Don't worry, honey."

I stood helplessly as he, too, climbed into the jeep. I watched as the wheels spun in the snow, as it turned and slid up the road. Then I realized Beatty's car was still there and he was standing near me.

"I said get out."

"All your protectors are gone now, girlie," he laughed nastily, striding back up the stoop.

A vicious snarl at my side caught him midstep and he backed hastily, his eyes wide. Merlin stood there, spread legged, snarling, no question of his intention. I don't know if Beatty would have drawn the gun he started for. I think he would have and Merlin might have died in the attempt but Regan Laird, his jeep skidding to a snow-splaying stop, changed the odds in our favor.

"I'll be back, girlie," Beatty warned me again and walked quickly to his car while Laird watched from his jeep. Once certain Beatty was on his way out of Pull-in Point, the major jockeyed the jeep into the garage. He slammed out of the car and to me on the double.

Despite his ferocious attitude, Merlin was barely able to stand, his side bleeding from exertion. I supported him as best I could until Regan Laird reached us and tenderly lifted the dog up.

"What in hell happened, Carlysle? Why were DeLord and Bailey in an MP jeep?" he asked as he gently pressed new gauze pads on Merlin's bleeding side.

I explained as lucidly as I could, trying to control both temper and tears although I was so stunned by the rapid succession of events I didn't think I was making much sense.

"They arrested Turtle and DeLord went with him to see what he could do. Said he had something to explain to the C.O."

"Beatty's favorite reading always was government mail posters. I guess he's added AWOL notices as his part of the war effort."

I stared stupidly at the major. "But they arrested Turtle for attempted homicide. . . ."

"Whose?"

"Warren's."

He didn't seemed surprised at the victim.

"That explains the AWOL then. I thought Master Sergeant Edward Bailey had changed character. The regiment always meant as much to him as it did to your father." Accidentally he pressed too hard against Merlin's side and the dog let out a cry, turning his head to lick the major's hand as if he realized the hurt was unintentional. Laird stroked the dog's ears apologetically. "I wish that vet would come. He's torn open the sutures DeLord made."

I knelt beside Merlin, stroking the muzzle he immediately buried into my lap.

"But what I don't understand, Major, is how they could *know* Turtle shot Warren?"

The major rocked back on his heels, looking me squarely, in the eyes.

"Warren could have seen Bailey take aim at him. To be honest, Carlysle, I knocked Bailey's gun up once when he'd a bead on Warren."

"Oh, no."

"It was just after your father's death when we had moved up on Setterich. Bailey and I were the only ones that knew your father had been killed by a forty-five slug. Bailey had been bitter enough at Warren when Emsh got killed and he took the colonel's death very hard. I thought he'd go out of his mind when DeLord came in with your dad. Christ, the heart went out of all the men. Bailey acted as if Warren were the Jonah for everything, from the losses of the Third Battalion at Bois de Collette to the beetfields right up to and including your father's death. But I checked Warren's side arm myself and it wasn't even clean, much less fired recently."

The major's eyes turned cold and bleak.

"I myself find it very hard to forgive Warren a few things. D'you know, he actually tried to assume command the next morning after we got back from the cemetery? Oldest in grade, logical choice. Hal I got through to Division and Gerhardt and scotched that."

I don't think I heard all he had been saying. I was so torn by the despair that had driven Turtle, in loyalty to his colonel, to desertion and attempted homicide. And his capture.

"How could Turtle get back here . . . to the States? He had no travel orders or. . . ."

Laird gave a mirthless chuckle. "After twenty-eight years in the army do you think a little thing like proper travel orders would stop Bailey? He probably forged them. And did a good job, too, I'll bet."

"It's awful, it's just awful," I muttered hopelessly. I felt limp, bereft, numbed, not even angry anymore.

He took me by the shoulders, only this time he held me gently and bent over to look in my face.

"I think I'd rather have you ranting and raving than woebegone like this, Carlysle," he said quietly. He tipped my head back, his eyes searching my face. "Damn it, girl, I can't keep on buoying you up with booze and knocking you out with seconal." He shook his head slowly from side to side. "But you've been clobbered good and often. As a guardian I'm doing one helluva poor job of it. Whereas you, short of mucking about with my socks," his voice quickened, "and, young lady, don't ever let me catch you doing that again; a laundress I don't need." He sounded forceful. "Is that straight?" and he gave my chin a punch. I jerked my head away.

"Yeah." His manner demanded an answer.

"As I said, you've been doing a pretty good job of taking care of me. Now, I brought in supplies and I think the best thing that could happen to what's left of this squad is to feed it. Right? I did go after coffee and food before this latest skirmish."

He paused at the door.

"C'mon, Carlysle. Lend a hand."

He said it in a way that precluded disobedience. My legs moved of their own volition and I followed him out to the jeep.

12

REGAN LAIRD WAS RIGHT to get me busy with the mechanics of daily routine. We fetched in the groceries and put then away. I noticed numbly that he had found Idaho baking potatoes, and this put me in mind of Robert DeLord and hi; mission. I put that out of my mind and washed and put the potatoes in to bake. I made a hearty meat loaf, vaguely wondering at all the stamps such a generous amount had taken. The major had brought in fresh cod and flounder but I was tired of fish. There were some fresh vegetables and oranges. I didn't examine the canned goods closely, except the dog food.

"I didn't have much choice for Merlin," the major said apologetically.

"I know."

We were both marking time until DeLord got back. l wondered idly, anything to think about but DeLord and . . . I wondered why Evans had been so certain a vet would come to this point off the coast of nowhere for any dog, much less a civilian's. The major busied himself by bringing in more and more wood and spending lots of time policing the fireplaces. I made beds and straightened rooms, pretending that Turtle's belonged to someone else. Then, as darkness was falling on the snow-bright world, there was no more busy work to be done. I sat down at the kitchen table near my dog and folded my hands in my lap.

The major came in with one more, unnecessary load of wood and shed his outer clothes.

"Say," he began as pulled up a chair to the table, "what did you find in the locker? Anything valuable?"

I looked at him blankly and then twisted around, wondering where the locker was.

"That's funny. It was here in the room."

"Yes, but did you find anything in it?"

"You just bet we did. Ancient bibles, hundreds of years old, some absolutely unique French Colonial stamps, and guess what was in those cartridge boxes?"

"What?"

"Jewels stuck in dud shells and a boxful of gold and jeweled crosses."

The major whistled expressively. I got up, peered out into the corridor, rummaged in the back porch, ducked my head into the study.

"I don't understand it."

"Think back, Carlysle. You say you went to the door? Had you finished with the footlocker?"

"Almost. Most of the stuff was back in for lack of a better place to put it."

"Bailey and DeLord stayed in the kitchen when you went to the door, then? Long enough to clear the rest?"

"I think so. But where could they have put it then?"

"Did the MPs come into the kitchen at all?"

I closed my eyes to concentrate. "I saw Turtle come to the door of the dining room, stand, crouch, turn, to be blocked by the lieutenant. Then the MPs came up, DeLord stayed in the doorway until Turtle went to get his coat from the back hall. One of the MPs must have gone with him but that's when Beatty got so nasty. Then. . . ."

"Beatty got nasty? How?" demanded the major and I realized I'd rehearsed that scene out loud.

"Just nasty," I said, waving aside his interruption. "Then Turtle went with them. No, I'd gone to Turtle but I didn't think to look in the kitchen. Yes, and the lieutenant showed them his papers and asked to come along. They agreed he could so he went to get his things. He took the Colt along, too."

"When I drove up," the major said thoughtfully, looking at me out of the one corner of his eye, "you were at the door, Merlin was snarling, and Beatty was on the front stoop."

"I'm only sorry Merlin was so weak," I said with regret.

"So what happened to the locker?"

"There was no one else in the house. No one came in the back because Merlin would have warned me."

"Well, somehow, between the time you went to the door and the time the MPs got in here, the locker got stashed away."

Merlin growled, his head up, ears alert. I let out a disgusted breath.

"Oh, now what?"

The major turned quickly to me, a half smile on his face.

"That sounds more like my ward."

We both went to check, of one mind on the advisability of screening visitors to this house. Merlin's growl rumbled after us and cut off with a yip.

"Down Merlin. Stay!" I ordered. He whined a protest but stayed.

A wood-paneled station wagon cautiously slowed to a halt on the snowy road. It appeared distorted, top-heavy. The slit lights went off and we saw the over-tall door open. No one emerged. The door hung ajar. Then a figure got out and seemed to keep on standing up like a cartoon drawing unexpectedly elongating. The door was closed and as the shadow of the tall figure separated from the shadow of the top-heavy car, we could see a familiar medical case swinging from the end of one long, long arm.

"The vet did come," and I think I was as surprised as the major sounded.

He hastily opened the front door and, for all his own six-foot odd height, he had to look up at the tall, tall man who entered.

"Major Laird?" an unexpectedly tenor voice asked.

"Dr. Karsh."

"Have we met?" and the voice was unusually musical with no trace of a down-east accent.

"No, but I've heard of you."

"Hmmm. Wouldn't doubt it for a minute."

Merlin barked.

"My patient is in good voice."

Merlin yipped because he had disobeyed me.

"Spoke too soon."

The veterinarian ducked under the archway separating hall and dining room. I backed up instinctively so as not to have to crook my neck to see his face.

"My ward, Carlysle Murdock. Merlin is hers."

"Quite a beast, I'm told. Twice told, young lady. Once by an excited coastguardsman of my acquaintance and once by a lieutenant, a calmer man but equally insistent that I should come."

He swooshed his bag at me to indicate I should lead him to his patient. I scurried ahead into the kitchen.

Merlin got to his feet and stood there, swaying slightly, the major's bandage bloody.

"Merlin, if you weren't so sick, I'd beat you. You were told to stay."

Ashamed, Merlin dropped his head, peering up at me with a woeful expression in his eyes. Then he jerked his head up, his jaw dropping as his dog face registered surprise.

"Ooooh," and the doctor's voice was a croon of delighted interest. "Now you are a magnificent fellow. You are indeed."

The doctor's voice was a marvelous singsong. He ignored us completely, heaving his bag to set it with a very soft plump on the kitchen table, although it must have been very heavy. Then he dropped to his knees by Merlin in a fluid movement. He didn't attempt to touch the shepherd but he bent this way and that so he could see Merlin's points in the undiffused kerosene light.

"What a dog! What a superb dog! Have you any idea, Merlin, what a sight you are to these tired eyes?"

Merlin was watching him, absolutely mesmerized.

"He's hypnotized Merlin," the major whispered, bending his head to my ear.

"I've never seen Merlin behave like this with anyone," I murmured back, not wishing to interrupt this significant meeting. .

Dr. Karsh placed his long-fingered hand under Merlin's chin, his over-length thumb stroking the soft fur of the muzzle.

Merlin's eyes drooped sleepily, his head leaning into the supporting hand much as a tired child will cradle himself against his mother. With his free hand, the doctor explored Merlin's body, the deep chest, the long back, the well-placed hips.

"Will you clear the table?" the doctor crooned, not changing his voice one decibel from the tone he was using to soothe Merlin. It took me a moment to realize he was talking to the humans in the room. The major and I jumped to his bidding.

With a deftness and speed that was an astonishing blend of individual motions, Dr. Karsh had lifted Merlin and placed him on his good side.

"The lights, so and so," the doctor directed, waving fingers at two distinct levels. We complied.

"Now, young fellow me lad, let's get a look at this outrage on one of nature's grandest. As the lieutenant said, his was rough field surgery but I think he did extremely well. It's only that you do not obey your mistress' order to stay."

The major and I found we had to pay close attention to this dialogue, delivered in a rippling Irish tenor-like tessitura, for sometimes he was talking only to Merlin and sometimes to us. The doctor had by now washed his hands thoroughly and donned rubber gloves.

"Now this will not be pleasant, my sagacious friend Merlin—a marvelous name for a magnificent specimen of *Canis familiaris*. I congratulate you, young Miss Carla," and he paused briefly to prepared his curved needle with black gut, "on your perspicacity in seeing in a bumbling puppy the dignity of the adult dog to come. Or perhaps you created a personality for him to grow up to. . . . Steady, this will hurt but not for long. There! Merlin is a sensible creature and knows that my hurt will cure. . . . By eschewing the Rover-Chief-Rin-tin-tin mania, you gave him a goal of wisdom to acquire. For Merlin was a great magician and there is magic in the heart of a dog when he will defend his against the mechanical madnesses of men. Oh, one more and the worst of my ministrations are over. You can do yourself no more damage, my silver shepherd. This wound will heal, given God's good time and what appears to be a superb constitution. There. Good boy! Not a word out of you. Brave lad."

Dr. Karsh straightened, having bent double to work, interminably it seemed to me, on his patient. The shadows of the kerosene lamps jumped around as his upward ascent caused a draft. The doctor took two long strides to the sink and stripped off the gloves. He had to stand sideways as he did not fit under the canopy across the sink. As I hurriedly got him a towel, still speechless, I realized I came only to his belt. I hastily backed away. Way up, he smiled down at me as he handed back the towel. Then he turned and scooped Merlin up again, depositing him on his quilts, giving the dog a stern signal to stay. Merlin licked his chops, whined very softly, rolled to his good side, sighed, and fell asleep.

Dr. Karsh stood staring down at his patient and, pivoting in place, favored us with his full attention.

"Evans was right to say I should see Merlin myself. I do not mean to imply," he hastily assured me in his mellifluous way, "that the dog is in any danger . . . no, no : . . not to deprive you of his company, but as fit mate for a lovely young thing of my own. I had despaired of ever matching her size and color, not to mention her temperament for she is, above all, amiable and affectionate. Evans knew at a glance that Merlin was the dog to husband her. I am grateful to him."

"I'd be willing, very willing, Dr. Karsh," I answered breathlessly. My voice, which I had always considered rather light and childish in tone, sounded unexpectedly harsh in contrast to his. "I'd be delighted. I never thought you'd actually come so far on such a miserable day."

"My dear, I serve the animal needs of this community and my patients rarely can come to me. They are not your pampered bench pets in shows. They are working beasts and when they are ill, they need me," he said simply. He started to leave. "My word, I am so forgetful. The lieutenant who called to add an unnecessary but concerned plea that I attend brave Merlin asked me to tell you he will be back tomorrow. He said to say that something unusual has developed that he must check out. I trust his cryptic message reassures you. His tone was confident. I know I remembered his phrasing right, once I remembered I was to tell you something."

"Yes, yes, thank you," I assured him, bemused.

He started to bend out of the room.

"Keep him as quiet as you can. And major, for his comfort, carry him outside soon. By morning, he'll be no worse for wear."

And he was leaving. The major and I started after him but, with his long strides, he was out the front door before we could cross the dining room. "He'll know when he's well enough to be active. Feed him what he wants. I'll look in later this week, never fear, to feast my eyes again on a fine, fine dog."

He said these last words as he telescoped back into his car. Both the major and I stood, half dazed on the front step, oblivious to the cold, as he drove off slowly, in second gear, up the snowy road.

"He's unbelievable," I muttered. It was the sight of my breath in the cold that broke the spell. I moved out of the doorway and the major closed it, hurrying me by the arm back into the kitchen.

"I'd heard about him but I didn't believe it until now," the major said, slowly shaking his head.

"Merlin just let him sew him up," I exclaimed.

"I think I would, too," the major admitted with a bemused chuckle.

"I can't get over Merlin just letting him. The man's a genius," I said dazedly, and went to check the dinner in the oven. "Did you notice his car?"

"What about it?"

"It was top-heavy."

"It'd have to be for that beanpole."

"How can you say that?"

"Don't get your back up. Stands to reason he wouldn't fit in a regular car."

"He doesn't fit, period. He's unique. You said you'd heard about him?"

The major had poured himself a drink, offering me one which I declined. He settled himself at the table while I set our places.

"He's one of the local legends."

"He hasn't got a local accent."

"Educated. I don't have one either and I've lived around here all my life."

I said nothing but the major obviously hadn't heard himself speak. Still he didn't have much of an accent.

"In Orleans?" I asked hastily.

"Summers. Winters in Waltham."

"And you'd never seen Dr. Karsh?"

"At a distance. Never been introduced."

"Are there other vets around

"No, just never had any reason to call one."

I stared at him. "Didn't you have a dog as a boy?"

He grinned at me and the expression, distorted by the scar, reminded me I had all but forgotten his wound. He sensed the distraction and his smile faded. He leaned back, his bad side hidden in the shadows.

"No," and his voice was flat with a return of the cold cautious neutrality that had marked his manner towards me until just recently. I felt ill that I had been so gauche.

"Maybe . . . one of Merlin's pups?" I tendered in a small voice.

He looked at me, quick to sense this obtuse apology for my unintentional offense. He thawed.

"I'm sorry, Carlysle. You didn't deserve that of me. I've come to understand, in a way I never would have before, why Karsh prefers the quiet life here where people are so used to him they no longer notice his extreme height. He's accepted in a community that would defend him to a man against outsiders' curiosity. And he is a downright genius with animals. I knew that long before I heard a mutter about his size." He took a long pull at his drink. "It was all so easy when I thought you were a boy. It wouldn't be wrong to bury you down here along with me for a few months. But it won't work out now!" He drank again, his mood bitter.

I sank into the chair by him, just listening because I couldn't think of a thing to say although there was much I'd've liked to say.

"I'll have to reopen the house in Waltham and get a housekeeper." A return to Waltham appeared to be exceedingly distasteful to him.

"But you've lived a long time there? Surely they know you," I suggested, implying that his friends and acquaintances certainly wouldn't avoid him because of his scars.

His lips compressed into a thin line and I knew I was wrong. He drained the glass.

"Oh! How could they!" I cried angrily.

His glass came down to the surface of the table with a loud crack. He splashed in more whiskey, moodily swirling it around the ice cubes.

"I never considered I was particularly vain before this," and for the first time in our acquaintance, he fingered the scarred side of his face. "But then, war changes a lot of values."

"You're going to Walter Reed soon and they'll be. . . ."

He glared at me, opened his mouth to snap something out, and stopped.

"They might even improve on the original," I suggested ruthlessly, suddenly conscious that sympathy was the worst comfort I could offer him. "Your nose is a bit too aquiline. While they're about it, can't they reduce that hook?" I reached over and tapped his very aristocratic nose disparagingly. "I think you might possibly be able to achieve a Robert Taylor, smooth, suave look of distinction. Or perhaps the rough-hewed Gary Cooper type. You haven't got the basic structure for Cary Grant, of course. And next time, do get a proper haircut. The length is disgraceful," and I flipped up the long hair that covered the baldness of the scar tissue.

His fingers caught my wrist in such a vise I thought he'd break bones. The anger in him was white hot and I glared right back at him, daring him, knowing the anger he would vent on me was anger suppressed from whatever hurt he had suffered elsewhere.

The fury drained out of him. He closed his eyes and shook his head, breathing deeply to disperse the inner tension. His fingers loosened but he didn't release my wrist. When he opened his eyes again, his face had cleared of both bitterness and anger.

"I'd forgotten an incident I should always remember," he said in a low normal voice. "When I was in the hospital out in the Newtons, a woman came into the ward. We were facial injuries, all of us. I was not the worst one by a long shot. There was a fighter pilot who'd had—" he broke off. "She was a good-looking woman and obviously had plenty of money. I remember she swept in with furs, smelling of fine perfume, every hair on her head in place. She was everything none of us wanted any part of. Not the way we looked. Well, she introduced herself and then proceeded to take off her hair, take out her teeth, and pass around photos of herself before and after her accident, before and after surgery."

He swallowed, his face still. Then he looked at me. "There wasn't a man in that ward, with the exception of that pilot, who wasn't better off than she had been. God, her face had been sliced and mashed cruelly. And there she was, looking like a goddamned junior league virgin. She spent the whole afternoon with us, talking. She made us feel her face where the grafts had healed, showed us the tiny scars in her hairline. She told us this could be done to us, too. And she said go ahead and make any improvements we wanted, just for laughs. When that lady left, every one of us stood up and saluted her. She didn't have to come, she didn't have to do what she did but she came often. There's all kinds of courage in the world."

He picked up my wrist in both hands and gently stroked the angry marks his fingers had made.

"Thanks, Carlysle, for reminding me of her."

"Any time," I said lightly, because I was embarrassed and flustered by his confidence. I felt I had learned more about Major Regan Laird in the past few moments than I'd discovered in the last few days.

Merlin stirred in his sleep, his feet twitching in the urgency of some dream sequence.

"God, I'd better get him outside," the major said, rising.

"When that's taken care of, dinner will be ready."

13

WHEN MAJOR LAIRD came back in, Merlin was walking stiffly beside him. Regan Laird's face was suffused with mirth.

"The poor damn dog," he chuckled as I looked at him questioningly. "That poor dog." The major sat down, trying to stop laughing.

Merlin moved to his bed with what might be considered injured dignity. He paid no attention to us, curled himself around and lay down again, a deep sigh forced from his lungs as he settled. He lay with his head towards us, blinked his eyes once, and then closed them.

"That poor damn dog," the major repeated for the third time.

"Enough's enough," I exclaimed for Merlin's sake.

"Dinner smells good," Laird said, controlling his amusement with effort.

"Learned this recipe from a gentle lady of good background but impoverished circumstances near Bragg," I explained, passing him the meatloaf. "Oh, and the lieutenant had missed baked potatoes so much."

The major covered my hand with his, giving a little squeeze.

"I'm just as worried as you, Carlysle, in spite of the doctor's message. But I can't change it by worrying about it so I don't. Takes practice but it saves a lot of wasted time and effort."

He cut a massive slice of meat loaf for himself. I was appalled at such liberality, being used to meatlessness.

"Eat, drink, and be merry, for tomorrow who knows?" I asked.

He nodded agreement so I helped myself to an equally huge portion, and we dug in with good appetites.

The events of the past few days had blunted quite a few sharp edges and sent several shoulder-carried chips flying. Tonight for the first time I felt at ease alone with Regan Laird and he was at ease with me. It was a nice harmonious feeling. I hoped it wouldn't be fragile, that possibly it could last a while.

I was surprised to learn that he had a B.S. degree from Boston University in civil engineering. He had joined the army in 1939 when he couldn't get a job.

"With typical army efficiency, they put me in infantry O.C.S." He grinned.

He had an older sister, married and living in Texas, but she was now his only relative, their parents having died several years ago. He had been married but he'd sued for divorce in 1941. I never learned more than that.

He had joined up with the First Army in the fall of 1941. He had met Dad and liked him but it wasn't until September of '43 that Dad had wangled Regan Laird's transfer into the regiment.

"Are you going to stay in?"

"I could. Retire at forty-one with full pension? Not bad. They'll have occupying forces for years when this is settled. Here and in the Orient."

"That's what Dad wrote," I put in eagerly. "I'm majoring in government. Dad is . . . Dad was sure he could wangle me a job as a civilian employee in the occupation force. My German's good and my French is fair."

"I got your midterm marks. You're a better student than I was," he remarked, proud, if vicariously, of my scholarship.

"Don't sound so patronizing," I suggested because I'd just figured out he was only twenty-nine, not in his mid-thirties as I'd assumed.

"The prerogative of my experience and position!"

"You're only twenty-nine."

"Thirty in June!"

"You make yourself sound ancient." I laughed at him. "Of course, you are," I added, "compared to the male population I'm used to."

"Really?"

"There's this math genius on the campus," I said with some

feeling, "who's not more than fourteen. So help me! He tells the math instructors where their errors are."

"That must endear him no end to the faculty."

"And he loves nothing better than to matchmake at dances."

"For you?"

I glared at my guardian. "He's exactly my height. And his best friend, for whom he tries to make a match, is a seventeen-year-old, pimple faced Latin scholar."

The major's eyes twinkled. "I think I had better get a chaperon. To protect me, from you."

"Go mend a fire!"

He left chuckling. I looked at the closed door, not the least bit annoyed. Rather I was extremely pleased. I felt alive again, and good, and somehow tomorrow *would* take care of itself. Even the terrible reality of Turtle's arrest and the grim delight of indicting Warren. The depressions that had plagued me, the indecisions that had worried could no longer overwhelm me.

I suppose I had been so badly put down by circumstance, there was no place to go but up. I couldn't attribute it all to having cleared the air and achieved a nice relationship with the major. But that helped. So did the curious magic of Dr. Karsh. The aura of his incredible personality seemed to linger although I couldn't have described his face, what color his coat had been, or even whether he had been dressed in business clothes or a garage overall. The impression he gave of immeasurable depths of kindness and understanding, for humans as well as animals, was more palpable than such details as color or texture.

I fixed some of the meat loaf for Merlin, justifying this extravagance as both reward for his heroism and a necessity for his convalescence. The smell of food under his nose roused him. As he ate, I stroked him lovingly, telling him how wonderful he was. He ate all I gave him but didn't look greedily for more. He laid his head on my shoulder briefly and then sighed very deeply, rolling his eyes to gaze at me wistfully.

"Okay, go back to sleep."

He curled around and settled back again. I busied myself cleaning up the stove. I sloshed the coffeepot to measure its contents. The sound was suggestive and the idea of more coffee was appealing.

I glanced over my shoulder at the step stool on the far side of the porch door, remembering the major's injunction. I wrinkled my nose disrespectfully.

I was levering myself up onto the counter when Regan Laird returned. He grabbed up the stool and marched over to me. He set the stool on the floor under my dangling feet. Spanning my waist with his two hands he picked me up and set me joltingly on the top step. His eyes blazed a few inches from mine.

"If I've told you once, I've told you a dozen times to use that stool. I don't want you breaking your fool neck."

"Stop sounding like a father," I snapped irritably, our previous rapport shattered.

"My feelings towards you at the moment are scarcely paternal," he retorted heatedly, his jaws clenched.

When he had encircled my waist, my hands had automatically gone to his shoulders for balance. Furious at his proprietary manner, I dug my nails into his shoulders.

"Why you little . . ." and before I knew it, he had hooked an arm around my waist, roughly jerking me against him. He wound the fingers of the other hand in my tangled hair and pulled my head towards his.

His mouth fastened angrily on mine. He must have intended that kiss as a disciplinary affront. But the moment our lips met, the moment I responded, his intentions changed. I could feel it in the tenderness of his mouth on mine, in the longing strength of his arms as they tightened about me. I had never been kissed like this before not even by the acknowledged lady-killer of Riley. And Regan was no less hungry for such caresses than I.

I found my hands were kneading the muscles along his

shoulders and back, gripping his strong arms in an instinctive desire to be as close to him as possible. My whole being was concentrated in the warm, hard pressure of his mouth covering mine, his hand burning at my waist, his fingers in my hair. Time was a curious new dimension of contact points that thrilled and ached as we clung to each other. Beneath my urgent hands I felt his body begin to tremble. Deep within him I heard a soft groan begin. Very gently, most reluctantly, he loosened the tight embrace. His face, a blur above me, became separate features, his eyes achingly tender and gentle as he searched my face.

My feet were back on the stool and he framed my face with his hands, one thumb stroking my temple where a frantic pulse beat. A very, very gentle smile touched his lips.

"Talk about surprises," he murmured in a husky voice.

He leaned forward again slowly, giving me time to evade him if I wished. He bent his head to kiss the base of my neck. I felt the rough scar tissue against the skin of my throat and quickly pressed his head against me, my lips on the wound by his forehead. I felt him stiffen slightly and then relax as his lips continued to move along my throat. He suddenly stopped, raised his head, and looked at me with a peculiar expression.

"I can't go on like this. I'm supposed to be your guardian, not your seducer."

I looked at him with what I hoped was a solemn expression but exultation surged within me.

"There is a way in which you may be both legally." I said and held my breath at the conflicting emotions that crossed his face. He started to draw back but I tightened my hands around his neck.

"Unless, of course, you've been trifling with my affections. . . ."

He gathered me tightly to him again, his lips against my hair, my head pressed against his good cheek.

"No, by God, I'm not trifling with you, Carla. But I'm a one-time loser already. I'm not a good husband candidate."

"If it makes any difference, my father didn't think so."

Startled, Regan tilted me in his arms so that he could see my face.

"How in hell do you figure that?"

"Why in hell do you think my father went to such asinine lengths to throw us together? I don't need a guardian."

Amazement flooded his face.

"Why the old—of all the crazy. . . . Oh, Carla, I'm in love with you all right enough. I know it's rushing things, but watching you cook, flounce around my kitchen . . . even your funny moods. . . . I was so mad when you washed my socks . . . I . . . I. . . ." and his lips covered mine which was what I wanted very, very much.

He kissed all kinds of ways that gave me intense delight. My pulses raced so violently I couldn't breathe. Then he set me very carefully on the counter and backed up to the table. He sank to the surface, rubbing his hands along his thighs, regarding me.

"That's enough of that for tonight," he said decisively. And, I thought, considering the sweetness of the moment, a little grimly. I knew what he meant for I was aroused and he surely must be.

"No nonsense now, Carla. You'll have to go somewhere else until we can be married. For a little bit of a thing you're much woman."

I beamed at him. "Only three days for blood test and license. I've got my guardian's consent."

"Three days! Wait a minute," Regan said, holding up a restraining hand. "I'm due down at Walter Reed."

I jumped down from the counter and, before he guessed my intention. I put my hands on his head and kissed his scarred cheek.

"I don't want anyone to say I married you for your good looks," I said softly, earnest despite the light tone. He remained so still I dropped my hands uncertainly. His eyes were closed and he held his head back stiffly. I could see the pulse in his neck beating strongly. Then his head came forward slowly as he expelled a deep breath.

Frightened, I wondered if I had offended him with my impulsiveness; if I had gone on one of my headlong plunges unaccompanied. Just when I was afraid he would never break the silence, he held his hand out to me.

"You unman me," he murmured and I shall treasure forever the look he gave me.

Hastily I placed my hand in his and we stood that way, just looking at each other. Slowly, after a very long moment, he drew me gently to him and kissed my forehead.

"If you don't leave me . . . now . . . Carla . . ."

I was half tempted to stay, fully aware of the consequences, when the rational part of me insisted this would be unfair to Regan's New England conscience. I was at the door when I remembered another obligation.

"Merlin!"

I saw Regan grip the table edge with both hands.

"Get out of here, Carla. I swear I'll take him to bed with me. I'll order him to guard me. But, Carla darling, don't let me hear your voice again until morning." The room echoed with the intense emotion in his order.

I really didn't want to leave but I did, closing the kitchen door softly behind me, the blood still hammering in my veins. When Regan did claim me, I wanted him to have no reservations, no dying qualms of guardianly conscience; a curious switch of conventional positions!

14

I WOKE the next morning, alert as I had not been in a long time, alert and eager for the day to begin. It was early in the morning for the sun was just up over the edge of the dunes sheltering the Point from Nauset Beach. My watch said quarter of eight.

The fire was almost out and I rose hastily in the cold to build it up. I smiled to myself as I realized Regan had not mended it as he had done every night since I arrived. His abstention endeared him further to me. Despite the chill in the room, I stretched fully and luxuriously, curling my cold toes up, away from the frigid floor.

I rummaged through my suitcase to see what I had to wear that was more appropriate to my improved status than pants and layers of concealing sweaters.

I had lost enough weight during the bout with strep throat to make both my wool dresses hang badly. Really, my wardrobe was sadly lacking in anything suitable. I had either skirts and sweaters for classes, cocktail and dancing length dresses, or pants. I had to settle on a kilt, Dress Mary plaid in red and green. At least the full pleats gave me some semblance of curved femininity. I had matching pullover and cardigan to wear with it. Quite British, but the garnet red of the sweaters lent a warm color to my face. As a concession to the unheated house, I tugged on knee-length socks and loafers.

I almost skipped down the stairs but restrained myself into befitting dignity. I'd be very quiet and sedate and have breakfast ready for Regan when he woke. But when I went to feed the stove, I found fresh wood just catching fire from the banked coals. Merlin was barking outside. Then the sound of water rushing in the bathroom warned me that Regan was already up.

Well, I could still get breakfast so I started fresh coffee. I sorted thriftily through the stale bread to make French toast. I had the table set when I heard Regan's steps in the hall. I felt myself blushing and I certainly experienced what was once termed "palpitations of the heart."

He was coming down the hall, he was at the door, his hand was turning the knob. I couldn't bear to stand there, barefaced, waiting so I whirled to the stove, pretending much industry over the spider. The door opened and he must have stopped at the threshold. Did I make the proper picture, I wondered?

"Morning," I said cheerfully without looking round.

The door closed.

"Breakfast is nearly ready," I added, making great work of turning the crisping bread.

He advanced towards me and then I could feel him so close that if I leaned a fraction backwards, I would have rested against him. Above the rich smell of French toast, I caught the odor of piney soap and shaving cream, clean linen and after-shave lotion, a combination excessively masculine and very stimulating.

Then his hands cupped my shoulders, his fingers tightening one by one. He bent and kissed the right side of my neck where the sweater ended.

"Now," he said softly, his voice rich with laughter and love, "let's see what my Little Bit looks like dressed as a girl?"

His hands turned me and so help me, I was suddenly too shy to look up at him. With one hand he pushed the frying spider off the burner. Inadvertently following the motion of his hand, I looked at him.

He laughed, deep in his throat. His eyes, more blue than gray this morning, were gleaming with good humor and affection. Still laughing, he spanned my waist with his hands and lifted me high. I gasped, grabbing his hands for balance before he set me down with my feet on the stool, his face level with mine.

"Now, try to avoid the issue," he dared and, turning his head slightly to one side, drew me into his kiss.

The kiss was no less thrilling than the anticipation of it. I wished I could just melt into him. I certainly tried to. This morning he was master of the situation whereas last night's encounter had been spontaneous. His attack on my senses was as deliberate as it was skillful. By the time he released me, I was the one trembling.

The expression in his eyes told me this was exactly what he intended and I quickly searched for some diversion to give myself a breather. My glance fell to his chin where he had cut himself shaving below the unshavable scar. As he saw my eyes drop, I felt his arms stiffen. The muscles of his mouth tightened into the thin line of withdrawal.

I wasn't going to put up with this. If I wanted to look at Regan Laird I was not going to have to put on blinkers until he'd had plastic surgery.

I put a finger on his chin and gave a little push.

"Something I owe to the soil that grew. More to the life that fed. But most to Allah who gave me two separate sides to my head."

Kipling was furthest from his mind at such a moment. He gave a shout of laughter, hugging me exuberantly to him, swinging me around and depositing me on the floor again.

"Message received, over and out. I'm hungry," and he gave me an affectionate shove towards the stove before he sat down.

Merlin barked at the back door and I let him in. He nosed his face into my hand in greeting. If his walk was stiff and slow, he was again operating under his own power. He went up to Regan, laid his head on Regan's knee to have his ears scratched. That attended to, he went back to his quilts and sank down with an enormous canine sigh.

"I took a look at the sutures this morning before I let him out," Regan remarked. "Doing fine."

"Anything else would be a surprise to me," I said with complete confidence in the skill of Dr. Karsh.

We had taken our time over breakfast, the problems to be met today remote from our talk. Regan was dressing to go for more wood when Merlin came alert, a bark in his throat. Regan glanced at me inquiringly.

"Friend, whoever it is," I said. "DeLord!" We both moved swiftly to the front of the house. A Navy jeep was idling in the driveway, but there was no sign of its driver. Just then there was a knock on the back door and someone hallooed.

Merlin barked twice. Evans, the good Samaritan, stood in the kitchen doorway, grinning down at Merlin who had walked stiffly over to greet him.

"Gee, miss, he looks so much better. Dr. Karsh get here?"

"He certainly did, Evans," Regan replied as he shook the young coastguardsman's hand gratefully.

"I'll have to revise my conditioned opinion of the Coast Guard," I remarked. "Particularly since you sent us that incredible man."

Evans' eyes shone. "Ain't he something magic? Say, did he like Merlin?"

"Love at first sight. Do you know he stitched Merlin's side and that dog didn't so much as flinch?"

"Believe it. I believe it," Evans assured us fervently. "Oh, Major. A call came in to the station for you. You don't have a phone, I know. I left the jeep running and we can make it back to the station in no time."

"DeLord, I imagine. I'll be right with you, Evans."

As the sandpeep hesitated, Regan ushered him to the door, closing it firmly behind him.

"Why'd you do that?" I asked, surprised at his behavior. It bordered rudeness.

"Because, my dear ward, I do not wish to complicate your position on the Cape any further by having the Coast Guard witness our passionate farewell," he said as he folded me into his arms. He lifted me clear of the floor, grinning broadly at the disparity in our heights.

"You'll have to wear those clog-heels like Carmen Miranda," he teased as he bent his head.

And a passionate farewell it was for we had not kissed often enough to be the least bit casual about it. We both intended to be brief but Evans revved the motor loudly and I was set on my feet so quickly I had to clutch the edge of the table to keep my balance.

"I'll need that cold ride," Regan muttered as he strode out the door.

By the time I had the table cleared and was starting the dishes, I had recovered my wits enough to start worrying. Regan had jumped to the conclusion that it was DeLord who had called. Well, if he had good news, why wouldn't he just come back here? I chided myself for being pessimistic. Maybe DeLord needed Regan's supportive evidence. No, Regan had been wounded before Aachen. Oh, I'd find out soon enough. No use borrowing more trouble until I knew there was some. Besides, it was difficult to stray long from the engrossing subject of Regan and me.

How incredibly delightful to contemplate the prospects. Oh, the dean was going to be livid. She hated married students. They were always giving birth in the middle of exams. We could live at the Waltham house and I'd take the summer session to finish my junior year. I assumed Regan would want me to get my degree. That was but one of the hundreds of things we would have to discuss. It was good I did have the rest of the term off at that. A nuisance to worry about a wedding and studies at the same time the way one of the girls had had to. Boy, was she a nervous wreck.

I was so wound up with projections that Merlin had growled twice before it registered as a warning.

"Easy, boy," I said for Merlin had risen. "Down! I'll go see who it is."

I carefully. closed the kitchen door to keep him in and preserve the warmth. I was still so bemused I didn't so much as glance out the dining room window. I even opened the front door wide. When I realized who my visitors were, it was too late to slam it. Beatty's foot was across the sill. Just behind him stood Marian and Donald Warren.

"Alone, Miss Murdock?" Beatty smirked.

I knew then that he knew I was. Fleetingly I wondered about the phone call Regan had gone to answer at the station. Merlin started to bark furiously. I heard his claws scrabbling on the kitchen door.

"Constable Beatty was kind enough to drive us out here," Lieutenant Colonel Donald Warren announced in that patronizing nasal voice I remembered all too well.

"You look so wan, dear Carlysle," Marian Warren said, insipidly correct.

Beatty firmly pushed the door wider and stood aside for Marian to enter. The three of them stood indecisively in the hallway. I said nothing.

"My, it's cold here," Marian Warren said pointedly.

Merlin barked continuously.

"Oh, I was hoping you didn't have that beast here with you," she said, shuddering delicately. "I hope you have him chained up. Donnie always swore he was vicious. He certainly sounds like it."

I glanced at Warren whose face had taken on that look of intense strain which proximity to Merlin always produced. In spite of that, Lieutenant Colonel Warren looked revoltingly fit, his wounded arm carried conspicuously in a black silk sling.

Warren was not an ill-favored man. His face was full, his features even, and he carried himself well. He looked the proper officer image and if you didn't know what an indecisive person he was, what little insight he had into anything beyond the end of his rather Roman nose or the pages of the Manual of Arms, you'd have been reassured about the quality of officers running the war. As a matter of fact, he looked more the model of the proper officer than my father had. The natural gauntness of Dad's rough face always seemed forbidding. Dad, although the same height and general build as Warren, appeared too thin, his tunic dropping from bony shoulders to a hipless torso. The comparison was even more distasteful to me now.

"Isn't there any warm room in this house?" Marian Warren

demanded petulantly, drawing her thick Persian lamb coat tighter to her.

She hadn't changed. She still looked skillfully plucked and painted. I'd bet anything she was wearing a crepe dress, floral pattern, under that coat. Naturally she wore silk stockings and had high heels on under the rubbers she wore as a concession to the unplowed countryside.

Merlin gave voice to unrestrained displeasure at the sound of her voice.

"Don't worry, Mrs. Warren," Beatty said, his hooded eyes glinting smugly. "That dog's too hurt to stand on his feet."

I didn't bother to contradict him because I felt I could handle Beatty without Merlin's help today. He wouldn't dare anything in front of the Warrens.

Another fact registered with me. Donald Warren was aware that Merlin was seriously injured. It was probably the only reason he had come under the same roof. He not only hated Merlin; he was terrified of him.

"Shut him up, Carlysle," Warren ordered through set lips, "no one can hear a word with that racket going on."

I allowed sufficient time to pass for Warren to realize I issued the command on my own, not because he ordered me to.

"I'm so cold, Carlysle," Marian Warren complained again.

"I'll light a fire in the living room," I said with no graciousness and continued with a bald lie. "The only other room we keep warm is the kitchen. And Merlin's in there."

Beatty opened the living room door, displaying a familiarity with the house that I didn't like. He strode over to the fireplace and knelt to light the fire.

"If Beatty would be so kind to light the fire for us," I suggested sarcastically.

The room was more than chilly; it was frigid. The clammy damp cold seeped through my double sweaters. I refused to budge from this room and ignored the desire to shiver.

"There. This fireplace draws well. Take the chill off the room in a sec," Beatty said genially.

"Unless your presence is official. . . ." I said acidly to Beatty.

"It is," Warren replied with unctuous mien. He planted his square body directly in front of the fireplace, hugging any warmth.

Beatty looked at me, a smirk on his mule's face. His eyes took in the fact that I was dressed in a skirt and sweaters. I inwardly cursed the fact that I had no protection from such insolence.

"I fear I am forced to exercise a most unpleasant duty," Warren continued. Beatty's smutty look was driven from my mind. "I must recover some stolen property from you."

"Stolen property? What stolen property?" I demanded.

"Oh, come now, Carlysle. You received your father's foot-locker and his personal effects. You don't imagine those parchment books and those valuable stamps are legitimate spoils of war? I know he thought to make restitution—"

"What are you talking about?"

"I told Division that I would handle the matter as tactfully as possible," His face lengthened with simulated regret. "There will be no publicity and, in view of your father's otherwise satisfactory record as an officer, this will be forgotten. But only if restitution can be made to the French authorities."

"What are you saying?" I demanded, the chill forgotten as anger rose in me—hot white anger at the snide implication in Warren's words. "How the hell can you imply anything so ridiculous?"

"Come off it, girlie," Beatty put in jeeringly. "You hand the stuff over and we'll leave. Otherwise I have a search warrant right here. You defy it and I'll have you in jail."

"Go ahead. Search. You won't find anything stolen here."

If Regan and I hadn't been able to find that locker, they couldn't.

"Come now, Carlysle," Warren snapped, his pose abandoned, "don't be tedious. We know you have all your things here."

"Because your second-story man couldn't find them at Mrs. Everett's?" I taunted.

"I told you she'd be difficult," Marian said.

"You're damned right I'll be difficult. The very idea of you two ghouls coming here, slandering my father when all the time. . . ."

My voice had risen in outrage and roused Merlin who began barking frantically, banging his body against the door.

"Shut that goddamned dog up," Warren bellowed, his face white, his eyes darkening with apprehension.

"Only because he's wounded and don't think I don't know who caused that," I cried. "Merlin, shut up!"

Merlin whined in protest, but he stopped barking and battering the door.

"Search the house, Constable," Warren directed Beatty in the offhand manner he used with anyone below his own rank. His manner did not set well with Beatty whose good opinion o' himself did not include subservience to anyone. I did not miss that quick flare of irritation as Beatty trudged down the back hall. As he passed the kitchen door, Merlin growled. Beatty cursed him but continued.

"Really, Carlysle, you're making a difficult duty very unpleasant for Donnie. Only the fact that your father served so many years with him persuaded Donnie he must intervene, for the reputation of the regiment. Why your father—"

"Spare me your interpretation of duty," I snapped. I never could stand the sound of that woman's voice; there was a whiny edge that grated on my nerves.

Marian Warren blinked at the outright animosity and looked appealingly at Warren.

"I'm distressed you're taking this stand, Carlysle," Warren said, switching to the father-confessor pose. "Marian and I wanted to spare you."

He appeared to deliberate, turning to his wife, shaking his head regretfully, shrugging his uninjured shoulder to show he had been forced into a difficult position.

"I have to tell her, Marian. Maybe then she will cooperate. After all, her father was only trying to shield the insubordinate sergeant of his—"

"What has Ed Bailey got to do with this?"

Marian Warren gasped, her mascaraed eyes wide. "She doesn't know?"

Warren's hand had gone significantly to his wounded shoulder. He wore a pained expression.

"We were called down from Boston yesterday to Camp Edwards to identify Bailey. I'm afraid, my dear," his reluctance was pure crap, "that not only did Bailey loot thousands of dollars of valuable stamps and irreplaceable manuscripts from German baggage trains, but he tried to kill me when I accused him."

"Stamps? Manuscripts? Bailey?" I repeated inanely, dimly realizing that Warren was harping on minor items.

"Your father must have realized it first, of course."

"Go ahead, Donnie," Marian spat out viciously, her cold eyes fastened on my face. "Tell her! It'll serve her right, the way she's acted towards us. Just as if her father were chief of staff . . ."

"My dear," and he had the nerve to come over and put an arm around my shoulders. I stepped aside, showing my revulsion openly. He stiffened, his eyes narrowing. "All right," he snapped, his voice taking on the same edge as Marian's. "Your father was murdered."

He paused to see what effect his words had on me. I stared back my hatred. He evidently mistook this for shock because he continued. "By none other than your precious Sergeant Bailey. And I have proof."

I couldn't help it. I laughed in his face. I laughed at the outrageous invention of it, leaning weakly against the fireplace.

"Don't you dare laugh at my husband," Marian Warren screeched, her sharp thin fingers digging through my sweaters as she jerked me around to face her.

"She's hysterical, Marian."

"She is not, the little bitch. She's laughing at you, you fool," and Marian Warren slapped me across the face.

It stopped my laughter but the look on my face dissuaded her against slapping me again. She lowered her hand just as Beatty came back into the room.

"There's a much warmer room just off the dining room," he said, his eyes sliding up and down my body.

"Did you find anything?" Warren snapped, without taking his eyes from me.

"No."

"Search upstairs."

His peremptory tone caused Beatty to hesitate.

"You deal with her, Donald, I'm going to get warm," Marian announced loftily. "The sooner we find what we came after, Officer, the sooner we can all leave this icebox of a house," and she smiled conciliatorily at Beatty. "This is all very upsetting for the colonel. I just know his shoulder is bothering him. Do hurry and search the second floor."

Those two left. I heard Beatty clumping upstairs as Marian's heels clattered on the hall floor. Merlin crashed against the kitchen door as she hurried past.

"You can't think me stupid enough to swallow that accusation, Donald Warren," I said, surprised at the dead calm I felt.

He began to smile unpleasantly.

"And if you think Division will believe such a tale about my father, from you, you don't know your reputation in the Fifth Corps."

His smile broadened. "On the contrary. There is incontrovertible evidence. The obliging lieutenant brought along the slug that the medic dug out of your father's body. It matches the one that wounded me. Both were fired from Bailey's service revolver which was taken from him when he was arrested in Aachen, and tallies with the number issued to him."

He spoke with such conviction that a cold uncertainty paralyzed me. It must have shown in my face for he smiled his toothy smile, showing teeth badly discolored.

He must be wrong, I told myself. Whose was the forty-five we found in Dad's locker? Turtle Bailey could not have murdered my father. That was impossible!

Besides, it was Warren who had done the looting. Turtle hadn't. DeLord had proved that. He was completely satisfied it was Warren. And Dad had known it, too. That's why Warren had shot him.

"Bailey escaped in Aachen. If he'd been innocent, why would he run?" Warren's voice hammered at me and then he shook my arm roughly. "Now stop protecting that murderer and tell me where those things are or I'll see your father's name smeared. He was shielding a looter. He knew, too, how much money was involved. He was obstructing justice. I'll see his name—"

"You try it, Warren, you just try it," I shouted, losing all control, "and I'll give that court-martial proof of the many times my father shielded your reputation, covered up your mistakes. I'll tell them what happened at Bois de Collette when you lost ninety-five men because you couldn't give a decent order to save your own neck. I'll tell. . . ."

His eyes widened as the impact of my words reached him. He raised his hand, palm flat, to clout me when Merlin's body lunged past me, knocking him to the floor. He screamed, a curiously high-pitched, womanish scream, terror-ridden.

"Hold, Merlin! Guard!" I ordered, grimly satisfied by the look of abject terror on Warren's wide-eyed white face.

Merlin crouched, one paw lightly resting on Warren's throat. He snarled, his fangs a scant inch from the man's chin. Warren moved once and Merlin's jaws snapped without meeting flesh. Warren lay still, his staring eyes never leaving the dog's menacing face.

"Hold, Merlin. Just hold!"

I heard the back door crash open and Regan was shouting for me. I ran for the safety and sanity of Regan's arms, slamming the living room door behind me, knowing that Merlin would keep Warren there until I heard from Regan's lips how absurd that man's charge was.

"Carla, Carla, thank God," Regan cried, embracing me roughly with relief. "The phone call was a fraud. To get me out of the house. Bailey hasn't shown up, has he?"

Marian Warren came stalking out of the study into the hack porch.

"Major Laird," she began imperiously and was effectively silenced by his look.

"Regan, they're saying awful things about Turtle," I cried, "and that Beatty man is searching the house."

Regan's face was grim, his eyes terrible.

"What's the matter?" I wailed. "Where is Turtle?" .

"He escaped. When I realized the phone call was a fraud, and you were here alone, I got suspicious. I called DeLord at Edwards. He was just leaving to warn us."

"Warn us?"

"Sweetheart, listen. Turtle is armed and he's . . . desperate. He's sick. He knocked the guard out when they brought his breakfast, stole a jeep, and is on his way here. He's after Warren."

"Donnie? Bailey's after my husband?" Marian Warren cried shrilly.

She barged past Regan on her way to the living room but he grabbed her and propelled her back into the study.

"You stay in there, lock the doors, and don't come out unless you're aching for a stray bullet."

As if to give added urgency to his warning, we heard distant gunfire. Evans, who'd been standing in the door, withdrew hastily. I saw his patrol spreading out, crouching low behind the slope of the land, seeking cover.

Marian Warren shrieked again and slammed the study door. I heard the lock click and her frightened squeals as she raced to bar the study's front door.

"Regan, please tell me what's happened?" I begged, pulling at his arm because he had turned to join Evans. "Warren was saying Turtle killed my father! That the bullets match?" I yearned for denial.

Regan gently disengaged my hands.

"According to DeLord, Warren is right. I hate to think so, Carla—"

"It isn't so. It can't be so," I screamed.

Regan jerked his head around at the sound of another volley and indistinguishable shouts. He dashed out the door. Beatty came striding into the kitchen.

"Now what in hell's going on here?" he demanded.

I stepped aside, gestured him out the door, too shaken to speak. As soon as he had barged past me, I grabbed up an old coat from the door and followed him out. There were more shots, from just down the road.

I could see distant figures spreading out, advancing purposefully, black against the scintillating snow. I could see the white smoke-blossoms before I heard the crack of rifle fire. Then I caught a glimpse of the running man, crouched low but all too familiar. Sergeant Edward Bailey!

The coastguardsmen opened up from their positions at the edge of the scrub bushes surrounding the house. Horrified I saw the sergeant's body jerk and spin, lurch with a second jolt, and then sink slowly to the snowy ground.

The rough shakes were icy beneath my hands as I backed against the house for support. I stared at the distant dark form in the snow until tears dimmed the sight.

Numbed and blinded, I closed my eyes. When I opened them again, I saw men converge on the sergeant's body. Saw them take it away in a jeep. Another car picked up the remaining men and started towards the house. Then Beatty came around the corner. I instinctively drew back but he saw me and halted.

"Well, your murdering sergeant got his. Now let's—"

"One more word, Beatty. . ." and Regan left the threat hanging as he thumbed back the safety on the thirty-eight he carried.

Beatty paused only a moment before he backed slowly away from me, standing at a distance. Regan, his hands gentle, led me back into the house and sat me at the kitchen table.

"'DeLord's coming," he said, his voice heavy and flat. ,

A jeep motor whined up the snowy slope to the garage. I wasn't sobbing anymore but my eyes were full of tears that wouldn't go away so that I couldn't see, but my other senses became excessively acute. Heavy boots banged against a metal running board. Men were tramping with grating sounds across the garage cement. The door handle rattled and the hinges squeaked as the door was opened. Cold air beat on my shoulders. There was a heavy smell of cordite from recently fired guns, wet wool, and sour sweat. There was the distinct feel of many people pressing in around the room and the air was close.

"I see Beatty got here. I gather he brought the Warrens," Robert DeLord said as he slid sideways into the chair beside me. "I missed them by a hair at Edwards and then had to help trace Bailey." He, too, smelled of cordite and cold air and snow. His cold fingers touched my arm lightly and, obediently, I looked up at him. His face was very tired and his green eyes sad. There was no trace of any boyishness right now.

"Bailey's dead, Miss Carla," he said gently.

I managed to nod that I understood him.

"He told me he had fired the shot that killed your father."

"No." I contradicted him flatly.

DeLord's hand tightened. "Yes, Miss Carla. But he thought he was shooting Warren. You see, he heard your father ask me to go get Warren just as he was called to check out the ammo and rations. He didn't hear your father call me back. Instead, Bailey found a good place for an ambush and when your father and I came along the road, he assumed I was driving Warren back, not your father to Warren.

"You see, Colonel Murdock had just had a call from HQ. I found out later it was to tell him that the bait, those stamps and one of the Gospels, had not turned up at Division HQ with the other liberated valuables. So your father had proof it was Warren. If only the colonel'd told me then . . . that it was Warren he suspected . . . but I do understand why he felt he couldn't confide in me until he had definite proof. And he was mighty upset when he called me back and said he'd go with me."

DeLord leaned forward towards me, his face anxious, his eyes begging me to understand. "Bailey was only trying to protect your dad. He felt that if he killed Warren, your father'd report himself to the base hospital and recover from the wound. But he knew your father would never leave the regiment if Warren were here, the way the men felt about Warren just then. But Bailey's been faking eyesight tests for years. Your father was the same height and general build as Warren and in the dark. . ."

"Bailey wouldn't have killed my dad," I repeated stupidly, unable to accept the truth.

Regan's arm came around my shoulders and I realized he had been sitting quietly on the other side of me.

"No, Carla, he wouldn't have. He was out to kill Warren. By mistake, he killed . . . someone else . . . someone he worshiped. It isn't far off the truth to say Bailey went into battle shock. He talked himself into believing Warren had actually fired the shot and he nearly talked me into it except I couldn't see Warren killing like that. But, in a way, Warren really was guilty of your father's death. If he hadn't caused so much trouble, Bailey wouldn't have been driven to killing him."

Emotionally I could accept that interpretation. Maybe later . . . when it didn't twist and hurt so much. . . .

"Turtle did shoot Warren?" I asked finally.

"Yes," DeLord confirmed. "And the attempt at Aachen was not the first one, either, was it, Laird?"

"No," Regan admitted. "I knocked his hand up once near Julich, and the lieutenant who replaced Garcia in Able Company told me he caught Bailey taking aim on Warren. Told me later he was sorry he'd deflected the sergeant's arm. We all knew Bailey hated Warren. I felt I knew why but I was only half right."

"Is it safe to come out now?" a muffled voice quavered into the dead silence that followed.

"God, I forgot her," Regan muttered, rising. "Yes, come out, Mrs. Warren."

We heard her slide back the bolt and then she peered cautiously out. When she saw who was grouped in the kitchen, she pulled the door wide and pranced out, her face suddenly as livid with anger as it had been white with fear.

"Well, who are you?" she demanded.

"Robert DeLord, ma'am," and the lieutenant had risen, the polite Southerner no matter what. "This is Regan Laird."

"Well?" she demanded her voice harsh. "Have you captured that maniac? Where's Constable Beatty? Has he found that locker yet? Where's Donnie?"

"Yes, where is Colonel Warren?" asked DeLord, exchanging a look over my head with Regan.

"In the living room," I gasped. "He's in the living room. He tried to slap me. Merlin's holding him."

"That monster? Ah!" screeched Marian Warren, her eyes bulging with terror as she ran, ungainly in the high-heeled galoshes. Regan and DeLord followed, breaking into a run at her hysterical shriek. There was a ring of horror, so unlike Marian's usual pitch, it snapped me out of the paralysis that held me. I ran to the living room.

"Merlin, heel!" I heard Regan order and then, more softly, "Colonel? Colonel Warren? Answer me, man!"

Marian kept on shrieking.

"What's happened?" I demanded, pushing past the lieutenant who had halted mid-room. "Merlin hasn't . . ."

Merlin hadn't done anything. That was it, I guess. But Warren's abject fear of dogs had. The colonel was in a fixed-eye state of shock, his face gray, spittle dripping down the side of his slack mouth as he lay on the floor. Merlin had scared him out of his wits.

As the two men got the colonel, unresisting, to his feet and sat him on a chair, Marian, still shrieking, ran out. She came back in, dancing in a frenzied rage, towing Beatty behind her.

"Shoot him! Shoot that mad dog. He'll kill us all. Look what he's done to my husband. Shoot him! Shoot him!"

Beatty did go for his gun. I threw myself on Merlin, keeping my body between the officer and the dog.

"That'll be enough, Beatty," Regan snapped.

"Shoot him! Shoot him!" Marian Warren kept screaming.

DeLord strode over to her and, muttering an apology, slapped her quickly and smartly on both checks. It effectively calmed her.

"If you have a radio in that police car of yours, Beatty, call an ambulance. The colonel's had a shock. And keep that gun holstered in my house!"

There was an authoritative knock on the front door.

"Come in," Regan shouted, without taking his eyes from Beatty's face.

"Colonel Calderone," DeLord said, waving in a wiry, Italianate man.

"Thank God you came, Colonel," Marian Warren babbled. "Everyone here's mad. That dog is, too. They've been mistreating me and just look at Donnie." Then she stopped, her hand going to her mouth as she absorbed the look of cold contempt on Colonel Calderone's face.

"You were right about the truck, DeLord," he said turning his back deliberately on the woman. "There were three slugs in the gas tank. We've picked up the men." He turned back to Marian Warren. "There are a few questions I would like to put to you and Colonel Warren." He looked at the passive figure in the chair. "Colonel?" he said, his face puzzled by the lack of response.

"Warren has gone into shock, Colonel," Regan said. "No doubt," and he swung towards Beatty, "due to the untenable position in which he finds himself."

Beatty was the first to drop his eyes. When he did, as if sensing she no longer had a single champion, Marian Warren began to cry softly. Beatty glanced contemptuously at her.

"I came here to recover stolen goods," he said stubbornly.

"Yes, where is that footlocker?" Regan asked, looking at DeLord questioningly.

A shadow of a smile touched the lieutenant's mouth.

"Under the woodpile, of course!"

15

"SHE SAID NOTHING to me about any jewels," was Beatty's angry comment later when Colonel Calderone took official charge of the illegal shipment.

"Of course she didn't," DeLord answered. "They could righteously turn all this over to the authorities," and he waved at the array of treasures on the kitchen table. "I imagine Warren would have innocently suggested he take charge of the service Colt and the ammo and return them to Edwards. And neatly retrieve what he was really after."

Beatty snorted, shuffling his feet. Neither he nor Regan looked near each other and he avoided my glances studiously.

"What'll happen to that colonel?" he asked.

"If he recovers," Colonel Calderone answered him, "he'll stand a court-martial."

"And her?"

"She's been an accomplice in armed robbery. The civil courts will handle her. After," and the colonel grinned mirthlessly, "we find out how much more of this sort of stuff is still unrecovered from grieving relatives." He held up one of the ruby-jeweled crosses, the stones catching fire from the sunlight. "I heard a part of the list one burglar was giving the sheriff. Quite a racket they had. Well, I'll take this, Miss Murdock, and be on my way. Coming, DeLord?"

The lieutenant glanced expectantly towards Regan who nodded.

"I'll be along later, Colonel, if you've no objections."

"Colonel," I blurted out. "About Turtle?"

"Yes, Miss Murdock?"

"He . . . had such a fine record. He didn't mean to kill my father. They had been together since 1917. I even lived with his family after my mother died. Does . . . do you . . ." I couldn't continue. I whirled appealingly to Regan, towards Robert DeLord.

Regan came around the table and held me tightly, looking towards the colonel. The man sighed, shaking his head slowly.

"The family will be told he died in line of duty. In a way, I guess that's the truth after what you all have told me. And considering what Warren and his wife were doing I expect I don't begrudge the sergeant that popshot at Aachen." He gave me a one-sided grin of reassurance. "Look, I'll do what I can."

"He was a murderer," Beatty growled, his eyes darting around the room suspiciously.

"I'd watch that talk, Beatty, if I were you," Calderone said in a quick, harsh voice. The man was not tall but there was a confidence and subtle strength about him that was more impressive than mere size. "Your nose isn't too clean in this affair. An officer of the law involved in receiving stolen property?"

"Receiving?" Beatty gagged.

"That would be my testimony if one word of the circumstances around Bailey's death ever gets mentioned in this county!" Calderone's words had the crispness of deadly earnest. "Good afternoon, Constable Beatty!" And Beatty left.

Calderone turned to me, his face reflecting sympathy.

"That'll settle his hash. Now, Miss Murdock, if Warren recovers there will have to be an investigation but courts-martial, thank God, are not public. That's all I can do for you and Bailey."

"Thank you, Colonel."

He raised his hand to his cap in an informal salute, gathered up the treasure, and left.

I leaned weakly against Regan, so terribly grateful there was someone to lean on I didn't have to be the brave little soldier anymore. I could be a grieving, tired, weeping girl. But, oddly enough, though the double tragedy of Turtle and my father was leaden in my heart, I was dry-eyed.

"It seems like such a terrible, terrible error," I said slowly. "It has to be corrected. It has to come out fair."

"Here, honey, drink this," DeLord suggested.

I looked at the cup of coffee he was offering me.

"So help me," he vowed, "there's nothing but bourbon in it."

Regan gently seated me. I had felt him go tense at DeLord's endearment and it penetrated my numb mind that he was jealous.

"Yes, it was a terrible, tragic set of errors," Regan said quietly, thanking DeLord for the coffee the lieutenant handed him. "Doubly terrible for you, Carla. Now take a good drink. It's cool enough to swallow. You look transparent." His brisk command was leavened by a tone rough with suppressed feeling. "If your father hadn't been such an honorable fool, trying to protect a worthless brother officer simply because they were classmates, maybe this whole fiasco wouldn't have happened. The colonel would sure as hell have transferred any other incompetent replacement so fast the man wouldn't have known his sergeant's name. But that goddamned Pointer tradition, honor and duty. . . ."

I stared at Regan, astonished and dismayed at the scornful vehemence in his voice.

"What's the matter with honor and tradition and duty?" I demanded, stung and hurt.

"There," and Regan smiled broadly at me, "that's better. I can't stand you looking like a woebegone elf." He encircled my shoulders and drew me as close to him as our chairs would allow. "Your father's dead, Carlysle, and don't ever for moment think I haven't mourned him and missed him. He was a great man, a real soldier and a patriot. There are very few of his mold in any century. Bailey's dead, too, but he courted death. Killing Warren was one way to achieve it and revenge his error about your dad."

"What bothered Bailey most," the lieutenant put in quietly, "was what you would think when you found out what had actually happened. He was a broken man . . . tired and old and bitter."

"He didn't really kill my father. Warren did," I said, when I could get words over the lumps in my throat. The tears just fell down my cheeks into my hand.

"Oh, Carla darling," Regan whispered, kissing my cheek. "We're both pretty battered around right now but, in time, the worst hurt heals."

"Oh-ho," DeLord drawled in an altered voice. "Have I been outmaneuvered?"

Whether he meant it or not, the absurdity penetrated my grief.

"Rank has a few privileges," Regan retorted quickly.

"Well," DeLord chuckled, looking at our faces, "that would have pleased the Old Man no end." He laughed again at our expressions. "I know. In Paris he was bending my ear either about Miss Carla—he always called you Carlysle—or you, Laird. I didn't get the significance until I met you, Miss Carla," and grinning mischievously, DeLord inclined his head graciously at me.

"Then, Bob, would you give me away, kind of in loco parentis?"

For a brief second DeLord looked startled. Then he smiled broadly.

"Miss Carla, it would be my honor. But unless you two plan on an early wedding. I might not be able to oblige. I don't know how long I can string out the wrap-up of this assignment."

"It only takes three days. . . ." I pleaded with Regan.

"Shotgun wedding, by God!" he complained dramatically.

"Wouldn't be the first time for you, I imagine," I teased coolly back, rewarded by the look of shocked dismay on the major's face.

"Why, you impudent little bit of a thing. It was no such . . ." Then Regan caught himself as he realized he'd fallen for the bait.

The noise had roused Merlin who barked joyously, wagging his tail and cavorting stiff-leggedly around.

"Ah," Bob DeLord put in tentatively, "would you mind, Miss Carla, if I fixed myself a little something to eat? I left Edwards in rather a hurry this morning and—"

"Holy Moses, it's nearly lunchtime," I cried. "You both must be ravenous. There's some canned soup. Will that take the edge off your appetite while I fix something more substantial?"

I flung open a cupboard door, standing on tiptoe to read the labels.

"That sounds just fine, Miss Carla."

I had both hands on the counter top to give myself a boost upward when Regan roared at me.

"James Carlysle Murdock, if I've told you once I've—"

"—told you a thousand times to use the stool," I finished for him, ducking guiltily and turning to grimace at my love.

As he swung me up to the top of the stool to kiss me, I had one brief glimpse of Bob DeLord, ducking his head to soothe the bullet crease with careful fingers.

Printed in the United States
1417400003B/199